VAMPIRE IN THE HOUSE!

By

Raymond Van Zleer

Order this book online at www.trafford.com
or email orders@trafford.com

Most Trafford titles are also available at major online book retailers.

Print information available on the last page.

ISBN: 978-1-4269-1782-0 (sc)
ISBN: 978-1-4269-1783-7 (hc)
ISBN: 978-1-4269-8487-7 (e)

Library of Congress Control Number: 2009938677

Trafford rev.   08/09/2016

 www.trafford.com
North America & international
toll-free: 1 888 232 4444 (USA & Canada)
fax: 812 355 4082

– – –

DEDICATION

To those who choose love instead of fear.
To true friends, past, present, & future.
Especially Family!
With Thanks & Love

– – –

Author's Note

Dear Readers,
Sometimes, it is possible to respond and this is one of them.
In response to feedback, questions, and comments, I have done a
minor rewrite. Same story. Better dressed.
I have added clarifications for readers young and old.
I changed the formatting too.
My hope and my goal is to enhance your reading enjoyment.
To save paper in the printed version, for the sake of the
environment, chapter headings are continuous, except when
orphaned at the very bottom of a page.
Small though this change is, it plays a role in making a difference
for our planet and for us.
If we all think this way, what a big difference it will make!
I thank all of you for your feedback!
Thank you even more for your support!
You are the magic that transforms writing into a labor of love.

– – –

CONTENTS

– – –

LOCOWEED SUPREME

It's true! Mom and dad brought her home.

They swear up and down and sideways and to high heaven and back, that Julie Wynn is their daughter and my sister.

Yeah! Right! I did not believe it at the time and though I know better now, I still find it difficult to believe. So there!

On the other hand, Julie is my sister and I love and care about her even if she was secretly switched by space aliens or something, because she is still family to the max.

Julie has mom's brown hair and dad's solid features and we look like brother and sister because of our faces.

Julie's face has always had the softness that passes for cute. Her brown eyes are closest to mom's mother, not brown like dad, while I got blue eyes from dad's parents and blond hair from dad.

As for build, I ended up having the willowy build from mom's parents, but Julie's is purely her own.

Small and petite like my grandpas each claim their moms were, yet blended with a stockiness that is unique to Julie because of what she has grown up to be.

In fact, the only things she has that are un-family are her soft sweet voice and her fangs, both due solely to her unique anatomy.

She also got mom's hands, slim and dainty, but dad's upturned thumbs snuck in there just like they did on me.

I suppose this proves that we are family, but looking back now, what really proves it to me, is that God gave us the right parents.

A mom and dad capable of surviving the two of us, who love us and have the smarts to say what needs to be said when it needs saying.

To me, this confirms the existence of God and documents that He does indeed work miracles, albeit mostly behind the scenes.

This is the reason I do not to fully believe in "only" the biological connection despite all of the genetic scans that prove beyond any doubt that mom and dad are Julie's parents.

Their DNA is so prominent in her that even hack scientists and long-shot hype artists have given up trying to make a name for themselves by trying to prove that a third party was involved.

That is, other than God for the Holy Bible says that without Him not one single thing was made, and every single thing means just that!

Everything without even one exception, including my sister!

Therefore, if you claim to take the Bible literally, then you cannot deny these words. However because I am family, I am free to believe whatever I want and what I believed then and now, is that Julie is different despite the DNA.

At the time she was born, I was only nine, so what did I know?

"A lot!" I insist and I really did!

I knew that when humans have a baby, it is supposed to be human. Not something else. But something else was what mom and dad knew they were bringing home.

When I said this to my best friend, Tom, who was also nine, he jokingly decreed that girls aren't the same kind of human as boys.

That changes nothing because my sister isn't quite the same as girls. Human girls that is.

Then again, maybe I am not quite the same either. That is, from the boy perspective because shortly after my sister was born, I told Tom: "In a couple of years we're gonna be dating girls, so why not be friendly with them now?"

He looked at me and said: "Yuck!" so I said: "It's either girls or gay," to which he retorted: "Sucky gross!"

I changed the subject to videos or something since there is no reasoning with someone when they are in puke mode.

Besides I have a relative who is openly gay, so I know that it is not something to panic over, though some fanatics do.

Even today, those fanatics still screech that the reason Julie was born into our family is because we have an openly gay relative.

They believe that if they decree: "That person is evil!" then their very loving, totally merciful, all forgiving God, will deliberately do mean and evil things to that person's distant relatives.

This sounds like something the members of an evil gang would do, so I ask: Does God really stoop that low?

I refuse to believe that He does.

Of course those same fanatics say many other crazy things too, like that my sister was born when the moon was full.

That statement is locoweed supreme because the new moon was on March twenty sixth, and Julie was born on March 29, 2009, when the moon was a waxing crescent heading into its first quarter.

That is why I am writing this book.

To tell the actual story as we lived it, versus the news snippets and fantasy stories floating around out there in Buymeland.

I am Leo Wynn and I was named after one of dad's best friends.

I never met the guy, but being named after him is better than being named after my astrological signs or the Plant X.

Mom is like way big into astrology, so she was a little distressed when I was born in the year of the Rabbit, because in oriental astrology, Rabbits and Roosters are supposed to be mortal enemies.

That suits me just fine because my dad is a Rooster.

Now that is just an excuse and I admit it!

Still, I am grateful that mom and dad did not name me Rabbit Wynn or worse, Cancer Wynn.

Why anyone would name an astrological sign after an illness was a mystery to me when I was nine, but I was already old enough to know that people do crazy things, like for example, my dad.

His name is Gerald, he goes by Gerry, and he still believes that selling cars is the ultimate way to earn a living.

Somehow he was able to earn a decent living by selling cars, but around the time Julie was born, money was leaner than watered down oatmeal.

That did not faze dad at all. Maybe because he is a Taurus, and it did not faze mom either, because she is a Capricorn born in the year of the Snake.

For some reason, mom gets along with dad just fine, though she is great with me and with Julie too.

Her name is Martha and she is into "it" whatever "it" happens to be.

Astrology is it. Selling strange and exotic things to all of her women friends and to anyone else, is also it. She has a collection of lighthouse pictures, miniatures, books, and posters of lighthouses that have fancy sayings like: "Let there be light!"

I assume this means that lighthouses are it too, and so is cooking special, great tasting meals, but mom only does this because these foods have something in them that makes us healthy or more intelligent or whatever.

Foods like carrots, broccoli, spinach, avocadoes, and artichokes, or whatever else mom once consider exotic and esoteric, so maybe Julie is what she is because of something mom or dad ate?

Much later, mom learned that these foods are not exotic, but the reason she felt that way, was because she was raised in a home where neither parent really cooked.

Opening a box, following the directions, then eating it according to the directions on the box, was and still is the sum extent of their cooking, so mom rebelled by teaching herself how to cook and by becoming involved in the finest "its" she could find.

At least mom did not name my sister after the oriental sign of the Ox or the month of March or the Aries sign.

I think dad first talked her into the name, Jennifer, because Jennifer was the mutual acquaintance who introduced them when they were in Junior College.

Mom was there because she had a cousin who lived near Los Angeles Pierce Junior College, allowing her to escape from her San Jose home in an affordable manner. Not because of parent problems but because she was feeling the need for freedom and she had not been ready to go to a university just yet.

She wanted a practical job she could depend on, no matter what, and her first AA Degree in General Education had led to jobs that were misfits, so she reckoned that a second AA Degree, this time in Bookkeeping, would give her a more personally meaningful job skill which she could use to work her way to a higher degree.

Then she met dad.

He had been selling cars for years and was at the Junior College to pick up some advanced skills.

At the time, mom was getting into numerology because to her it is like astrology: "It simply tells what is out there so you can use it like a mirror to see what's right or needs fixing. It is not fortune telling and those who use it for that are only fooling themselves."

Mom is not into palm reading either: "Modern chemicals muck up the lines. Some create them, some cure them, so unless you are Sherlock Holmes, forget it!"

Anyway, she was pleased with the results when she added up the numbers for his name and birth date in conjunction with hers.

Western and eastern astrology also gave positive readings and the calculations decreed: Good numbers, good planets and stars, despite the fact that each of them was born on the nineteenth.

Hence they were on or near the cusps of their respective signs.

In astrology the word "cusp" refers to the period when the signs are changing from one sign to the next, so mom decreed that she was ready for a change and married him, and later, dad told me: "Your mother takes life so literally that she is fun to be around!"

Agreed, and the one thing I have to say about mom is that she is true to her sign. She takes life so seriously and at face value that she is sometimes funny too.

As for dad, he is the proverbial bull in the china shop. A Taurus with just enough Gemini to give him a way with words. A man with the body of a miniature linebacker and an affable smile, who when

4

he was nine, decided that he wanted to be a car salesman and did everything needed to become one.

At sixteen, he handled the private sale of his parent's car and by eighteen, he was working at a dealership in Canoga Park.

Grandma Jean Wynn later told me how grateful they were that their son's only interest was selling cars, so they did not have to spend their time protecting the rest of their belongings from his need to learn and practice his trade.

Let it also be known that dad enjoys Chess and mom does not have a clue about the game: "If you want the other player's king that badly, why not just exchange colors?"

Mom is not into cards either. Especially not Tarot fortune telling cards, but she loves classical music and like dad, she really enjoys reading the Holy Bible.

As for mom and dad's beliefs, they are deeply held and they freely speak of them, but they never attempt to impose or force their beliefs on anyone. Not even me and my sister because to them, conversion is God's business.

They understand the Preaching of the Gospel to be by example and by actions based upon the teachings that Jesus commanded his followers to live by.

Not by arguments, dogmatic assertions, or verbal distortions, all of which are the basis of theological conversion.

Of course, biblical self defense is another matter.

So too is prayer, but I will not bother you with ours at all.

First because if you pray, you will know how and when we did it, and why!

Also because prayer is a private matter between each individual and God.

By the way, there is a reason for telling you all of this.

It better explains who we are and why we reacted the way we did when Julie came into our lives.

JULIE'S UNSUCCESSFUL DEATH

I became Leo because I have so many stars and planets heading to and through that sign's house that mom could not astrologically deny it when dad wanted to name me after his childhood friend.

However, mom did warn him: "Leo only adds up to a five. Since Gerald equals eleven and Gerry is a ten, he will be more combative and argumentative with you, than if we give him a more numerically powerful name... like Hilbert."

Dad much preferred Leo and I do too, and Penelope was the name mom wanted Julie to have if she was a girl because it added up to eighty eight and her predicted birth date and time could potentially bring some very favorable and impressive numbers into being.

But then, dad noted that less common names can sometimes be a liability for a girl, so mom did the preliminary numbers and charts for a late March birth and decreed that the child's moon would likely be in the wrong place for Penelope, but Jennifer would likely work.

The understanding was that mom would confirm the astrology and numbers after the birth, before finalizing the name.

Just like she did with me.

So my sister was born and the first thing she did was confound the doctors. Partly because mom did not believe in using ultrasound to scan babies in the womb, so this was not done, enabling Julie to catch them by surprise.

Mostly because they thought she was going to die.

The initial reason was that her mouth and throat are not connected in the manner normally seen in humans: Mouth opens and things head for the throat, but not in Julie's case.

For her, there is no opening leading to her throat.

Instead there is a valve that lets air out which is why she can speak, but not breathe in through her mouth, nor can she swallow things, and when the delivery room doctor saw this, he rushed Julie to the MRI scanner for a Magnetic Resonance Imaging scan in the hope that surgery might save her.

This was when the doctors discovered that her insides were more incomprehensible than her throat.

The scan took less than an hour.

The initial assessment took minutes.

A more complete diagnosis took days.

The final assessment including genetic testing on Julie and my parents, took over a month and understanding took several years.

Julie has a heart that is bigger than average, but it is not swollen.

It is just very big and even more powerful.

She also has a mass in her belly that looks like a giant sponge and two diaphragms. One for her lungs. One for her stomach and there were two holes in her gums where incisor teeth normally come in.

Vein-like tubes from these holes go directly to her stomach.

Julie's mouth, ears, and nose, look normal, but each has internal structures that are blatantly different, like a separate breathing tube that connects her nose to her lungs. Also, her tongue is raspy, which perplexed the doctors since there seemed to be no purpose for even having a tongue, given the lack of a throat.

Hence a tongue that was raspier than a cat's initially led them to decree that whatever genetic malformations had occurred, were more illogical than the words used by law-and-order politicians to justify and promote their ongoing criminal conduct.

As you know, the doctors eventually realized that Julie's genetics were anything but illogical, like her tongue, which she uses to clean her teeth in a manner no toothbrush can match.

But this knowledge came later.

Much later.

Equally belated came the realization that Julie's bone and muscle connections outwardly look typical, but the way they are actually internally connected is more than just notable.

Intensive studies have verified that her muscles and bones are beyond far more powerful than human, and they are unique like her eyes.

Again, a casual glance reveals little, but her irises are actually different, as are the dark openings that let light into her eyes.

Her irises are non-reflective and her pupils are more akin to an owl or cat, yet no animal biologist, animal anatomist, or veterinarian, has ever seen anything like those eyes or for that matter, like her.

Julie's most unremarkable feature is that she looks precisely like what she is. A girl. But internally there are differences which the doctors made a fuss over, speculating mightily as to what such things might mean, before finally concluding that this difference would not matter since there was no way Julie could survive.

With no means of getting meaningful food into her stomach due to the lack of a throat, she was going to die of starvation, assuming that thing in her belly even was a stomach.

Since nothing surgical could be done for her, on April fourth, the doctors told my parents: "When you feed her, she appears to be sucking in milk through the holes in her upper gums.

"Therefore, you have two choices.

"Leave her here and we will care for her as best we can... or take her home and give her your love and comfort. Either way, she will eventually die... so do what is best for you and your family.

"The only thing we ask is that you let us examine her while she is alive, and please donate her body to science. Our hope is that the knowledge we acquire will enable us to one day save others.

"We are working on a grant to cover the medical examinations and issues that your insurance company refuses to cover."

Mom and dad chose to give Julie the love and care of family, ordered me to be a loving big brother to my little sister, and brought her home.

However, during the time when the doctors were running their tests and searching for arcane explanations and clues, mom was too.

After learning about the medical concerns, mom had done the numbers and horoscopes and the results were mixed.

The astrology was unexpectedly favorable, but the numbers for the names were not. Yet even more, my parents wanted an expendable name that would not offend anyone in the family: "Why did you name a dying child after your beloved...?!"

Also, it needed to be a name whose numbers would not impose unnecessary woes on us, the way my ongoing conflicts with dad were, nor stigmatize its future use in our family.

So nominations were requested and dad suggested: Skye.

I said: "Julie," since a girl named Julie was giving me a hard time in school, naming my dying sister after her seemed fitting.

Because the overall numbers now worked out just fine, my sister became Julie Skye Wynn.

Saving grace was that our home was in California, because folks there are generally more tolerant.

Just to prove how dicey the situation later became, here is an example of the lunacy that the fanatics boxed us and themselves into via their belief based accusations and hatred.

If my sister had converted to the religion of one of those fanatic groups, the others would have accused that group of selling out and becoming avowed servants of Satan, so none of them wanted to openly convert her.

Secret conversion, sure, or publicly converting just the rest of the family, sure, but not Julie. Thus living in an area where fanatics were less of a pestilence was a blessing, but don't bother going to that house because the fanatics got it.

I suppose they needed to feel successful about destroying something.

Actually, the men who did the evil deed were from out of state and they also bombed the house at the other end of the block because my friend Tom and his parents just happen to be black.

Thankfully no one was home when the bombs exploded and the damaged houses were rebuilt, though the insurance companies refused to pay for those repairs, claiming that acts of terrorism are not covered.

This includes terrorism committed by American fanatics, so if we had been living there, our insurance would not have protected us either and this has nothing to do with skin color.

My family's skin color is white of European ancestry which proves that when it comes to finding excuses not to pay, insurance companies do indeed discriminate equally against everyone.

It is called Exclusions and Fine Print.

By the way, white is a color so if you are white, that means you are colored.

Of course back then, we were blissfully unaware of such things.

We had no clue as to what was actually going to happen when mom and Julie came home from the hospital, late in the morning on Saturday, April 4, 2009.

Not midnight on April first, like the fanatics keep claiming.

Just for the record, Julie was born at nine in the morning.

Not midnight. Not even at night.

To mom's credit, she insisted on staying with her baby around the clock and had told the doctors: "If you want to study her for longer than an hour or two at a time, you will have to keep me here with her. Otherwise I will take her home and we will come back for visits."

Mom knew her rights because her parents, Brenna and Brandon Lee were claims representatives in the medical insurance industry.

They knew the laws inside and out, and mom had learned those regulations thanks to the general shop talk she had overheard while growing up.

Therefore the doctors kept mother and baby in the hospital until ten a.m., then spoke the fateful words and had my parents sign the release of liability papers, so no one could sue the hospital or the doctors after Julie died.

I listened to the fateful conversation and watched mom and dad sign the forms, since my parents wanted me to be part of this meeting so I could hear the decrees and decisions.

Afterwards we headed home which was located on the eastern side of Santa Maria.

It was a typical house in an atypical city because Santa Maria was too big to be ignored, too small to be noticed, too strategically positioned along Highway 101 to be out of the way, yet it was unable to compete with the powerhouse small cities of San Luis Obispo to the north, and Santa Barbara to the south.

Its population of over one hundred thousand, still ranges from migrant farm workers, to doctors and executives.

They live here due to affordability and if they work here, convenience. Some who work in Santa Barbara or San Luis Obispo counties, like this area's housing prices and everyone accepts the fact that this city is among the windiest in the United States.

It is rural enough to be surrounded by farmland and it even has a few lingering farms within city limits, surrounded by greedy developers anxious for a quick dollar.

However, it was the winds and the outlying farms that would soon cause an uproar that would rattle the entire world.

Again, that was in the future because back then, mom and dad were bringing Julie home to die.

At the time this confused me a lot.

Not because I was nine, but because she showed no signs of dying anytime soon.

She was content to nurse and be bottle fed and her output soon became stinky enough to make all of us grateful that we could open the windows during the day and quickly blow the stench out.

During this period, we cursed windless days and nights and dad put up a tarp so mom could change diapers out on the patio, even on those occasions when it rained.

As for the doctors, they concluded that Julie was not getting the kind of nourishment she needed from her food, giving rise to digestive issues, spelled: Stench.

Soon, we learned that limiting Julie to breastfeeding decreased the stench, bottle feeding increased it, and my sister continued to defy expectations by not dying.

Grandparents, uncles, aunts, cousins, friends, and neighbors, all came by to give us advice and support, and to pray for a miracle.

The request that "God's Will be done" was the most popular prayer except of course for me and my friends.

We were taking a wait and see approach. Especially me because at the time, I did not think that having a baby brother was a good idea, so being stuck with a kid sister appealed even less.

But I did not actually wish death upon her, and the fact that she was supposed to be dying, meant that I should not have had to pray for such a thing anyway, even had I been so inclined.

Thus it happened that about six months after Julie came home from the hospital, Tom and I were playing when he noted: "For someone who is dying, she's taking her time..."

I shrugged: "Mom says that when she grows too big to suck in enough food, she will stave to death."

"Unbelievable! She looks like other babies except maybe a little smaller."

"Yeah. Mom says she's small for her age, but that's all. She looks around and hears things too, but if you hold her too near your neck, she tries to suck on it."

"Only the neck?"

"Dad says she does it cause she cannot reach anything else and cause when we hold her, she can rest her head on our shoulders, so our necks are right there."

"Non-cool! I was hoping she might be a vampire!"

We both grinned with glee and I agreed.

Neither of us knew how right he was, but the first clue actually came to light during this period, literally, when Julie began protesting being outside during the day.

Even on cloudy days, Julie would howl and fuss and mom discovered that she quieted the second she was inside a building.

Mom then told the doctors and they had her take Julie in and out of the medical building several times while they watched.

Their diagnosis was that my sister was hypersensitive to sunlight because she was dying and it was too much for her.

Just like sick people who need quietude and dimness.

From then on, walking the baby outside became a nighttime affair and life became more than just interesting, for by December, when Julie turned nine months old, she could do more than just crawl.

Thanks to her muscles, she could easily climb out of her crib and playpen, which made things a might bit traumatic for mom and dad since she was now a confirmed night owl.

She slept during the day and awakened just after sunset, then spent the entire evening happily playing, wanting and demanding company and she was enough of an escape artist to get her way.

Soon thereafter she began refusing to sleep in her crib.

During the day, she would climb out, crawl under the crib, then go to sleep and putting her in the crib after she was asleep changed nothing.

She would wake up soon thereafter and head back under the crib.

Since beds on the floor were rejected unless they were under the crib, the day after sister's first birthday, mom had dad clean and modify the unused doghouse that our dog, Tiny, had been avoiding like the plague since the day he had come to live with us.

11

Then out went the crib and in went the doghouse and Julie was content to sleep in it.

Thanks to the hinged door-like wall dad had just installed, removing the mattress and changing the bedding was far easier than a crib's, and the newly made thick flat roof served as a table.

Still, this new addition to my sister's bedroom made me suspect that my parents were finally becoming as eager for the medically decreed ending to come, as I had long been.

Primarily because the doghouse had been cleaned, but not painted, except for the new additions which dad simply clear coated.

In addition, he was storing the doghouse roof in the garage for future restoration, and this was when I began overhearing the word "normal" in some of mom and dad's wish statements.

It was a wish we were not granted and the first to learn about it was the family dog.

TINY THE PUREBRED SHEPADOR

Tiny had been a part of my life like since forever.

He was a Labrador-Shepherd mix who had the size and build of a small Shepherd with the coat and sweet temperament of a shy Lab.

He was seven and a half when Julie was born and by then, he was starting to look like rust speckled chocolate.

He also had an arthritic left hip that made him limp when he walked or ran.

Tiny came by his name dishonestly when mom was looking for the dog she believed was mandated by my recent birth and our family's astrological signs.

Numerological analysis had impelled her to pick one particular dog breeder over the many others who advertise in our local newspaper.

Since dad did not care what the dog was as long as it had four legs and barked, mom's tactics and needs were acceptable, so off they went. Mom's only requirements were: "It has to be good with children and when full grown, weigh under thirty pounds."

Mom really did not care about the weight, but the stars or the numbers apparently did. This allowed the breeder to decree: "I have just the dog for you! He is the runt of the litter so he will be smaller than the others... and since he is a purebred Shepador, his temperament will be perfect!"

Mom played it straight: "A Shepador?"

"Shepador is the breed you get when you mix a Labrador and a Shepherd. Both are great with kids and this little fellow has the best of both! You will adore him!"

Dad knows less about dogs than mom, but what he does know is spot-on because his job depends upon knowing thousands of inconsequential tidbits with unerring accuracy.

The reason is that salesmen need to be knowledgeable and credible, so if they blow it on the latest sports scores or dog facts with someone who knows the subject inside and out, that error could cost them a sale.

Thus dad was able to note: "Last I heard, Shepadors are not recognized by the AKC and both Shepherds and Labs average over sixty pounds."

In the United States, the AKC, the American Kennel Club, is the official decreer of which dog breeds are pure and which are mutts.

Still, this breeder did not miss a beat: "That's why I recommend the runt of the litter. He will be the smallest of them all... and the reason he is a purebred Shepador is because his father's a Shepherd and his mom's a Lab. Besides, if he was AKC registered I would have to charge triple for him."

Tiny's hefty dam whom the breeder belatedly named Wisp, was easy to verify because she was right there.

Dad noted that she was decidedly more than seventy pounds.

A picture of the sire, a Shepherd supposedly named Tiny Tim, was partly retracted when dad noticed that the name handwritten on the back of the photo was Godzilla.

The breeder backtracked a little: "Wrong photo. Godzilla is Tiny Tim's littermate. Tim was the runt of the litter too," but this no longer mattered to mom.

Holding the pup, she wanted to know: "What's his name?"

"I named him Tiny because he is so much smaller than any dog I have ever bred."

Over the years, mom and dad sometimes quibbled over the fact that Tiny grew to be "a little over" seventy pounds, and whether he even came close to being the smallest puppy in the litter.

What had mattered was that he licked mom's hand several times, then had the common sense to stop, yawn, and snuggle.

The timing was as perfect as his actions.

Thus Tiny had gotten his name and become part of our lives, and he was on the receiving end of whatever me and later my sister, could dish out.

So it came to pass that at five thirty in the morning on Monday, May 17, 2010, mom was heading to the kitchen to start the water boiling for tea and oatmeal, before checking on the critters, including me and the baby.

She later admitted to being frazzled due to having spent most of the night with Julie, then having to drag herself back to full wakefulness to get me off to school.

This explained why she reacted the way she did when she entered the living room and discovered the dog lying only partly on his dog bed, for neither parent believed in crating dogs even though Tiny made a dash for his crate whenever he got into the garage.

He loved that crate and the few times that we thought he had escaped from the house or yard, we had found him dozing inside of it, which was why dad had taken its door off and why we always made it available in the garage.

For us, it was good insurance against a runaway dog, but on this morning, Tiny had the martyred expression that only a dog who has lived its life enduring young children, can truly perfect.

He felt this way because Julie had somehow gotten him half way out of his bed and he was more than just trapped.

He was helpless.

Julie's right hand had a firm grip on Tiny's right foreleg. This same arm, her two legs, and body weight, pinned his forelegs, keeping him floored on his right side, despite his struggle to free himself.

The thirteen month old girl's left arm braced his head so he could barely move, while she contentedly pressed her mouth against his fully exposed neck.

However, what confused mom even more, was that Julie was humming in a manner unlike anything she had ever heard.

A calm pulsing trill seemed to be coming from very deep within Julie's throat.

In a fit of belated action, mom separated my sister from the dog.

As she picked up the girl, two things happened.

Tiny raced to the garage entry door, begging to be let out.

Julie, who was now nestled on mom's shoulder, went for mom's neck, humming softer than before, but still humming.

Mom let the dog out, surmising that Tiny wanted the safety of his crate. Then she headed to the kitchen, strapped the girl into the highchair, and set to work.

Soon water was boiling and there came the sound of the blender mom used to mix the baby formula, vitamin supplements, and mommy additions, that went into the cup my sister now used with mom's help because feeding was no longer easy for her.

After drinking Julie would tilt her head forward trying to open her mouth wider before belatedly remembering to close her mouth, then pull in the liquid.

Closing her mouth while sucking in the liquid seemed difficult for her and mom reckoned this was due to the fact that she was beginning to weaken, despite what she had just done to Tiny.

Soon thereafter, the sun climbed into the morning sky and Julie made the complaining fussing sounds that indicated her need to go to bed, so mom put the girl in her doghouse for the day, then she worked to get me out the door, and dad too, since he was manning the showroom floor this morning.

During breakfast, mom's only mention of this incident was her offhanded comment that Julie had been hungrier than usual.

The other hint that something had happened was Tiny's refusal to leave his crate.

Dad finally yanked him out and hauled him to the backyard.

This day was otherwise uneventful until nightfall when Julie crawled forth and made a toddling beeline, straight for Tiny, who raced to the garage as if his life depended on it.

Thwarted by the closed door, he again begged to be let out.

Dad obliged and the dog raced into his crate as fast as his arthritic left hip would allow, with the baby in belated, but determined pursuit.

This time, dad intervened, picking up the girl who howled in outrage until she was at shoulder height.

She then went for his neck, contently sucking on it, making the soft humming sounds mom had heard that morning.

Carrying his daughter into the kitchen, dad shared what had just happened and mom noted: "She did the same thing this morning. Her hunger is obviously increasing."

To mom, Julie's increasing hunger meant that she needed more calcium and magnesium, so mom added more of this supplement to Julie's formula and gave the blender its usual workout.

Julie drank it down with the expected struggle and when she wanted no more, it was daddy and brother time until we went to bed.

During this time, mom napped and dad awakened her when he finally bedded down for the night.

Forcing herself back to wakefulness, mom went to the bedroom where dad had left Julie. The girl was not there and following her instincts, mom headed to the living room where she again found Julie contentedly sucking on Tiny's throat.

The expression on the dog's face confirmed that he had given up and given in, so mom left the twosome where they were and headed into the kitchen to exercise the blender.

GOING FOR NECKS MEANS SHE'S HUNGRY

Tuesday morning at the breakfast table, mom told us about Julie's interest in Tiny's neck and suggested that dad put the door back on the crate so Tiny could have some nighttime peace and quiet.

She then instructed: "When she chases the dog or goes for our necks, that means she is very hungry, so tell me immediately."

Dad wondered: "Why the dog's neck?"

"Cause she's a vampire?" I inquired hopefully.

Mom sighed in frustration because she wanted me to have a good relationship with my sister and these ghoulish words were not it: "It's just a phase she is going through. She will outgrow it... assuming she lives long enough..."

I sighed and countered: "But mom! She does it on all her stuffed animals and on her dolls and on us too!"

This was easy to verify because the fur on the necks all of her stuffed animals was thoroughly munched.

The necks of her dolls were less marred but obviously munched, enabling mom's remark: "At least she is consistent... when she is hungry..."

Now it was Dad's turn to sigh: "The doctors said she would be suffering like this. Hungry... unable to appease it... so if sucking on necks comforts her... then that is something we can do for her... and what we will just have to live with."

He suddenly turned to me: "Just don't tell Tom or anyone else, unless you want them to tease you mercilessly."

I did not sigh, but I did grumble: "Tom knows. He's seen her stuffed toys and seen her chewing on them too, but he's golden. He's not telling cause that kind of story would get him laughed at... and the meanie kids would call him stupidstitious or something, and accuse him of making up stories."

This ended immediate concerns for everyone except the dog, who gratefully accepted the crate in the garage.

My parents tried placing the crate in the living room next to the dog bed, but this did not work because Julie would toddle or crawl over to the locked door, try opening it, then howl in outrage.

So the girl got fed, the dog began spending peaceful nights in the garage, and mom no longer had to guess when Julie was hungry because her beeline to the garage confirmed her need and intent.

This kept things under control until Friday evening, May twenty eighth, when the obligatory visit to the hospital took place since on this month, the twenty ninth was on a weekend.

The evening timing was in deference to Julie's sensitivity to sunlight and her need to sleep, since daytime was when she did it.

These once a month visits enabled doctors from six different specialties to loosely monitor her progress and each conducted their own examinations.

First came the baby exams, which mom later told us went as always, with the doctors shaking their heads over the fact that she was still alive and thriving and doing so well.

Afterwards, mom comforted Julie while the doctors asked questions and took notes.

Since Julie responded to the stress of these examinations by going for mom's neck, mom pulled out the formula she had prepared.

After it was warmed in the microwave, the doctors watched and video recorded the feeding, studiously noting and assessing her forward leaning, opened mouth response, then her struggle to close her mouth and suck in the liquid.

This was when mom told them: "Julie started going for the dog's neck so I upped the calcium-magnesium supplement in her food."

The rationales linking Julie's intense desire for Tiny's neck with supplements, needed an explanation, which mom provided at face value, along with her observation that increasing the calcium and magnesium seemed to lengthen the time between feedings, while lessening the frequency, but not the speed and determination with which Julie crawl-toddled after the dog.

This left the doctors wondering if they could now stand before God on the Day of Judgment and genuinely claim that they had heard it all.

Of course they already knew about her sleeping under the crib, but then came mom's "doghouse bombshell" because she had forgotten to mention it in April: "Julie was snuggling tighter and tighter to the wall, so I figured sunlight sensitivity was the problem.

"The doghouse eliminates that problem and positioning its door away from the window makes a difference too. She now sleeps the day without fussing and she is more relaxed and rested when she awakens."

These pronouncements, from Julie's single-minded pursuit of the dog, to putting a doghouse in her bedroom so she could sleep in it, slightly fazed the doctors who managed to keep their faces professional as they agreed: "It cannot hurt."

They then surmised that they might have indeed heard it all.

They also wondered if their creditability would be tarnished or tainted if they noted these parental observations and assessments in their ongoing reports to the agencies whose grants were funding their Julie studies, and to relevant medical journals.

To their credit, they submitted everything mom said, but on this evening they offered something new: "Since she is thriving, you have two choices. Continue the feedings as they are and up the amounts the way you have been doing, or you can switch to one of the prescription formulas used by those on liquid diets.

"Our reason for not offering this sooner is because it is exceedingly expensive and it is normally only prescribed for limited periods."

Mom chose to stay with what she was doing, but asked the doctors to determine how much of the cost, the insurance would cover and for how long.

This led to the idea of seeking grant monies to test liquid food formulas which was certainly acceptable, so while we waited for the grant to be approved, mom, dad, and I, continued sacrificing our necks and living with the nightly churning of the blender.

All the while, Tiny fervently sought refuge in the garage.

Nothing changed until the Monday, August thirtieth, evening medical appointment.

For us, it began with dad helping mom excavate herself and Julie from the car. He waited until after Julie's feeding ordeal, before asking: "How did it go?"

Knowing that the answer might effect me, I listened as mom provided the details: "She's ahead of where she would be if nothing else was happening. Her ability to walk and manipulate things, and her word usage... are closer to what is seen at twenty two months, versus seventeen months.

"So too are her neurological responses, so in those things, she is above average and we are being credited for doing things right.

"For keeping her alive and healthy too.

"As for her ongoing fascination with Tiny's neck... they know of no medical rationale that explains it... or why her sensitivity to sunlight has become so strong that we've had to move her doghouse into the hallway... or why she sometimes cries in pain when hallway doors are opened on sunny days.

"This level of sunlight sensitivity is something they have never seen or heard of, and the other thing that confuses them are her teeth.

"They appear to all be coming in at the same time... rather than individually and the doctors are worried about her incisors.

"They are growing where the feeding holes are, so if they block the holes and she has trouble feeding, those teeth might need to be pulled.

"As for the liquid formula. The testing grant has been approved!

"She will sample each brand for two weeks, then be put on the one that works best so the doctors can study its long term benefits.

"Since this is a medical study, the grant will pay for it.

"In exchange we are required to visit the doctor weekly to assess the results and pick up the formula we will be using that week."

This was wonderful news due to the realities of medical insurance.

Medical insurance companies were only in business to make money for the wealthy elite who owned them.

Not to pay for the medical services that the insured were paying those companies to cover.

For this reason, mom, with help from her parents, had been fighting tooth and nail to get the routine, non-grant things covered as much as they had.

Thus this grant meant that mom had one less battle to fight and the blender would hopefully be relegated to a less arduous existence.

Our other hope was that a potent formula would mean fewer feedings so we could stop using the latch dad had just installed on the door leading to the garage.

A latch mandated by Julie's recent ability to turn handles and open doors, enabling her to pursue the dog into the garage.

Since both our front and back doors had deadbolts, these were sufficient to keep her inside.

So too did the ceiling high security latch on the sliding glass door to the backyard patio.

Thus things were semi under control or as Tom decreed: "You now have the creature features to tame the savage beast!"

We all agreed, not realizing how wrong this assessment was and how soon we would have to live with those changes.

CASTLES AND COFFINS

The issues that kept the adults preoccupied in early September of 2010, were Julie's increasing intolerance to daylight and her teeth.

Noticeable only to those of us who were around her most of the time, was the change in her humming.

It was becoming more complex and soothing with each passing day, and even Tiny enjoyed it as long as Julie kept her distance.

However, the teething side of things was a little problematic since she was feeling the need to bite, but only soft things.

In short order, several stuffed animals and two otherwise indestructible dolls designed for teething toddlers, lost their heads when their necks disintegrated from the kind of withering onslaught they were never designed to withstand.

Still, despite fanatic rumors to the contrary, Julie never bit people.

I know because mom and dad held her a lot and I held her often, as did all of our family and friends.

None of us were ever bitten, though she did suck on our necks whenever she felt hungry.

It can also be said that all of the formulas were equal.

Julie needed fewer feedings but for her, the issue was taste.

She tolerated them but did not like them. Her face revealed her displeasure, but she drank them and hummed appreciatively on those occasions when mom made a batch of the old stuff.

These realities did not change the fact that she still wanted to open her mouth and lean forward to suck the liquid into her feeding holes and she had no way of telling us what she did not like about the formulas because she was only a year and half old.

Besides, words like sweet and sour meant nothing to her back then or now, because she cannot eat or taste such things the way we do.

Anyway, she drank the formulas, continued to thrive, and began growing an impressive set of teeth for her fangs were growing along with the others.

All were currently the same length top and bottom which evoked no comments beyond noting the incisor holes that enabled Julie to continue feeding.

Therefore the ultimate issue became sunlight and by Thursday, September sixteenth, it was more than just problematic.

Even though dad had added insulation to the doghouse, then piled more insulation around it, this had only provided a week's worth of comfort before more was needed, which helped only a little.

This was when I accidentally came to the rescue during a breakfast discussion.

Mom entered the dining room and said what we had been expecting: "She's starting to feel it again. Tomorrow she will hurt unless we add more insulation."

"I can try adding more," dad offered: "But the last addition protected her for only two days... so this will be it unless we insulate the house. The doghouse cannot support the additional weight and even if it could, doing so will block the hallway. Of course doing just the roof will be expensive and it will take time too... especially if a permit is required."

This was not good news, for money was tight and the current blockage was already making it difficult to get down the hallway to our bedrooms and the main bathroom.

In response, I mumbled: "Since vampires like to sleep in dungeons and basements, maybe a castle or basement would work?"

Mom snapped: "Leo! Julie is not a vampire!"

Dad ignored my remark and commented on my idea: "In this region, the soil is predominantly sand, so finding a house with a basement would require more than just a miracle... and even if we did find one, we could not afford it unless we won the lottery."

Mom wondered: "What about a room made of stone?"

I butted in: "I'd rather have a castle!"

Dad shrugged: "It's worth a try... but she would have to sleep in the garage since that is the only flooring in the house that can withstand the weight of that much stone."

I butted in again. This time with glee: "Tiny would love sleeping in the house again! We could give him Julie's room and she could have the entire garage all to herself!"

The idea of exiling or at least confining my sister to the garage, appealed to my eleven year old fantasies, but mom had a different take: "Insulating the garage would be easier and cheaper than doing the house and heating would be minimal since she sleeps during the day when it is the warmest."

Since my grandfather is a stonemason who specializes in hard stone like granite and basalt, dad noted: "A larger version of the doghouse is definitely affordable, since my father can make it and I can help."

He then utilized knowledge he had learned from listening to his father: "If it is a freestanding stone structure with no built in amenities like lighting or heating, it will not need permitting... and it will be far cheaper than adding insulation to the house... assuming that would even work?"

Mom concluded: "At night, Tiny can still sleep in the garage."

Mom's remark put an end to my dream of exiling my sister to the garage, but the need to have the stonework done as soon as possible, impelled dad to call his parents.

Since grandpa Terry Wynn had just finished a contract and was free, he and grandma Jean drove up from Reseda, California, that same day.

By Friday evening, the needed blocks and slabs of granite were sitting on our driveway, and in the garage was the specialized mini-loader grandpa Terry owned and used to do the needed heavy work.

Also there was the welding equipment and the metal rods grandpa insists upon using to reinforce every stone structure he builds. Even gazebo pillars, garden ponds, sheds, and play-houses, because California is earthquake country.

Thursday evening, dad finished clear coating the wood used for the flooring and on Saturday morning, the work began.

By late Saturday evening, enough stonework had been completed for my sister to use it on Sunday morning, the nineteenth.

Julie's hum of pleasure as she fell asleep was the only confirmation we needed and the finishing touches were added while she slept on a mattress deep inside of it.

Her total freedom was pain allowed mom and dad to put a hold on the roof insulation, but to my chagrin, her new bedroom ended up looking castle-like, rather than the ugly stone box I had smugly envisioned when the initial plans were discussed.

Even so, it was not decorative beyond the beautiful stone crosses grandpa made by patterning the layered stones in each outer wall and in the entry hallway and inner room too.

He did this partly because he was making it for us and because in everything he does, he strives for perfection.

Due to the smoothness of the stonework, it was never painted and naturally, we nicknamed it "the castle."

The rounding of its corners was done for structural integrity and to ease the use of chains should we ever need to move it.

Its hallway entry had a long sharp "L" bend to keep all light out and this was when we learned that Julie felt absolutely no need for any lighting at all.

She never bothered taking a light in with her, no matter how dark it was and she never asked for the garage lights to be turned on.

Not even when Tiny was there and she was looking for him.

For major lighting inside of the castle, dad had cleaned up his old portable mechanic's light.

Its shielded casing and hanging hook made it ideal for working on the innards of a car and for looking into the distant recesses of unlighted attics. Its electrical cable was long enough to circle and fully enter Julie's ten foot square stone sleeping room.

Thus it was as usable, safe, and foolproof, as the hand crank camping lanterns we used when entering the castle during the day.

Indents and peg holes in the castle's two foot thick walls were there for hanging the mechanic's light, our lanterns, a simple wooden cross, and whatever Julie might someday want in there.

Finally, there were two light blocking vent holes.

One in the three foot thick roof and one in the one foot thick floor, so air could circulate.

Since the light plugged into an electrical outlet in the garage, no special electrical wiring was needed and the same was true for the heater and a fan, but Julie never used them because heat and cold did not bother her at all.

Instead, mom was the one who brought them in and turned them on and off, until she realized that her child was not cold and threw off the blankets and sheets even during winter.

Mom then left well enough alone and there were no further issues.

We knew this because the entrance was large enough for adults to easily enter single file and also thanks to an FM monitoring system that allowed mom and dad to see and hear all from the comfort of the house.

Finally, if needed, more stone could later be added to thicken the walls and roof.

This meant that the only problematic "castle issue" was that Tom and my other friends wanted to play in it as much as I did.

Unfortunately, we could only do this after dark, when my sister was not sleeping in it, so we did, but only rarely because we could not leave things in it and we had to cleanup the mess we made.

Also, the low four foot ceiling was only fun for short periods and the fact that it was inside of the garage and had only one entry and no windows, made it even less fun. Even when playing submarine. Of course the real downer was the FM system since my parents could listen and watch anytime they wanted.

Thus my dreams of castle conquest were soon forgotten, but not having to worry about disturbing my sister on weekends was cooler than I had envisioned. Having the hallway back to normal was also a pleasure and when it came to Julie issues, these were now limited to speculations about her teeth and her feeding needs.

By this time, guarding Tiny was definitely a challenge whenever he was in the house at night.

For our sanity and the dog's too, a deadbolt had just been installed on the garage entry door, so the dog could sleep in peace.

A similar lock on the garage side door and another on the massive garage door, assured that no childhood wanderings could occur without parental supervision, while a shed in the backyard now stored what had formally been consigned to the garage.

Concurrently, mom and dad finally figured out how to arrange their schedules to accommodate Julie's needs and still have a life of their own.

What made this possible was that dad was really very good at selling cars and not just due to his extensive knowledge and gift with words, for he was the kind of salesman who put customer satisfaction ahead of a sale.

If a car was not precisely what the customer wanted or needed, he would explain: "I would rather you wait and buy the right car because if you are unhappy, I will lose a future customer and you will be wasting your hard earned money on an unwanted car.

"In addition, you will lose even more money if you sell or trade it too soon after buying it... so I suggest that you wait and buy the car that is right for you."

Thus over the years his reputation had spread and now that fuel efficient and hybrid-electric cars were being made available by the automobile corporations, those who had money were buying again.

This allowed dad to shift his schedule to meet customer demand in a manner that put him on the floor almost daily without being overworked.

Here, I should note that this is something a beginning or unknown car salesman cannot do since this job is usually strictly commission.

If dad had not had repeat customers who were asking specifically for him, he could never have done this, but since he could, it gave him time at home in a manner that enabled him to share the nightly vigil.

It also meant that dad had more time with me, enabling us to patch up our differences and find exciting new sources of conflict.

So leave it to Tom to sum up the situation: "A man's home is supposed to be his castle, but yours is in the garage and you can't use it cause a vampire's sleeping in it."

I grinned back: "A vampire is not vampire until it has a coffin."

Having lived with my sister's unsuccessful death for so long, I was more than just comfortable with gallows humor.

I was flaunting it.

At least when adults and parents could not overhear me.

Thus when Tom suggested: "Maybe we should build her one?"

I countered: "My parents will skin us alive if we do... and yours will too!"

"Then it's a go?"

"You bet!"

What we did was gather hefty cardboard and taped it into shape using an exterior framework made from the wood left over from projects our dads had undertaken.

Using felt markers we wrote "Coffin" and "Vampire Special" on what little cardboard was still visible.

We got the shape right but our supreme accomplishment was putting a tarp over it, to hide it from my parents.

Then came the hard part: When to sneak it into the castle?

We selected Sunday evening, October thirty first, because it was Halloween.

We began by coaxing dad into giving us some castle time.

Once in the garage, we snuck it into the castle and set it next to the mattress, its open lid resting against the wall.

Soon thereafter we went to a Halloween party and since the coffin had not yet been discovered, we called it night.

In the morning as we walked to school, Tom asked: "Did they find it?"

"Yeah. After Julie went to bed, mom checked on her and exploded... cause she climbed in and closed the lid!"

"Sweet!"

"Sweet and awesome!"

"Max! You grounded?"

"Two weeks. Mom's mad cause she thinks making fun of someone who is dying is majorly non-cool... and she's mad cause the lid had no holes. If dad had not said that there were more holes in the sides than Swiss cheese, I'd be toast."

"Did you tell on me?"

"No. Dad knows cause some of the wood and cardboard and tape are not ours and you were the only one with me in the garage last night."

After a moment, Tom asked: "Did Julie squawk when mom put her back in bed?"

"No. As long as sunlight does not bother her, she sleeps through almost anything mom does."

Tom paused, then smiled: "She closed the lid! It was worth it!"

"Yeah!"

JULIE DISCOVERS CHOMP NECK

Tom was also grounded for two weeks and we had to apologize to Julie, who was too young to understand what the fuss was about.

She responded by dropping the toy stuffed-cat whose cloth neck she had been chopping on, then she toddled off in search of the dog.

Father immediately hauled her to the kitchen, zapped the latest formula in the microwave, and offered it to her.

Little more of interest happened until the end of November, when Julie's incisors first began becoming fang-like.

The initial question was: Why were her incisors now lengthening?

Had her other teeth had stopped growing, or were her incisors now growing far faster than the others?

The other issue was that these incisors were uniquely sharp and exceptionally strong despite the presence of a feeding hole in each.

Each incisor hole was and still is grooved in the tooth's backside at the tip, then it funnels into its core, but what is puzzling is hole size.

These feeding holes are smaller than the holes in her gums, yet Julie was clearly getting enough nourishment despite the fact that closing her mouth during feedings was even more difficult for her now, than it had been before.

Finally there were some medical murmurings because the incisors should have been causing wear marks or cut marks on the lower teeth and gums, but nothing like that was seen.

That is, when the doctors and the dentist who was now part of the medical team, could examine them, since Julie did not like having her mouth examined and reasoning with a twenty one month old, who can move with stronger than normal speed and strength, and whose very sharp teeth are clenched tight, is the kind of battle few win.

To their credit, the doctors wanted to keep visits pleasant to foster future cooperation, so they kept their examinations quick and brief.

Then they took the long view.

After all, Julie would likely live to see her second birthday and her language level was above average since the number of words she knew was closer to the level seen in children two years and older.

Still, her word usage was sometimes confusing, like when one of the doctors, Susan Galt, MD, asked: "Why do you chase the dog?"

"Dog smell."

"What does the dog smell like?"

"Like food." Julie replied, her toddler naturalness implying that the adults are asking questions that have self evident answers.

Since her answer was not even remotely self evident, the next question was a given: "What does food smell like?"

"Like Tiny."

Thanks to this obvious dead-end, the subject changed: "Do you like sleeping in your castle?"

"Yes."

"Why?"

"Sunlight no hurt."

"How does sunlight hurt you?"

"Sunlight hot."

"Do you like the darkness?"

"Yes."

"Why do you like the darkness?"

"No sunlight."

"Is it easy to see in darkness?"

"Yes."

"Do you see better when mommy and daddy turn lights on?"

"No."

"When mommy and daddy turn lights off, can you still see?"

"Yes."

"What do you see?"

"Mommy and daddy."

Julie's attention turned elsewhere and this conversation ended with the doctors knowing that they had acquired valuable information that would need further clarification before understanding dawned.

What neither they nor we knew, was how soon understanding would come, while for Julie, the next big event was Christmas.

Since no one knew if or when the end would come, family and friends pooled their resources and bought Julie a large stuffed giraffe and a horse, each about the size of Tiny.

They paid extra to have the necks majorly reinforced which was necessary given how long and sharp Julie's incisors had become.

She immediately sank her fangs into each as it was presented and her hums revealed how much she enjoyed these gifts.

Soon thereafter, Julie's arduous struggle to close her mouth while feeding, confirmed for us, the timeliness of these gifts though the rationales for giving them were miles from the reasons she actually needed them.

Family also made a point of not forgetting me and the pod and new computer were beyond awesome.

Still, what we remember most, was that during this Christmas holiday season, Julie created a new game.

Chomp Neck.

The name was her creation but she had learned the word "chomp" thanks to me because I had long been playfully teasing her using variants that linked the words "Chomp" and "Neck" like: "Are you chomping on a neck again?"

Thus the name was really my doing, but the game was all hers.

After spying the alluring neck of a stuffed toy, or reclining person, or the dog, she would sneak towards the intended victim as fast as she could toddle, which was fast indeed.

However, she would freeze motionless if she thought she was being watched, or if what she was stalking, moved.

It was the length of time that she could stand statue-like without moving a muscle, that captivated us.

Dad timed one motionless stretch at over ten minutes and only belatedly realized that she had actually been covertly inching forward during a small part of that time.

Just when was hard to tell because she had been so still and moved so slowly.

This sneaking continued until Julie was close enough, then she would pounce with a hum upon the intended neck.

If it was a stuffed animal, she bit.

If it was human, she sucked on the neck.

The dog refused to wait around long enough to see what would happen.

One moment, all would be calm, the next second, we would hear a yelp.

If we were quick, we would see Tiny fleeing as fast as his arthritis would let him, dashing away from the humming opened mouthed toddler who was too close for comfort.

Mom or dad would then intervene and offer Julie food, while whomever was free, comforted Tiny.

The only problem now was that sometimes, Julie was not hungry.

This was great news since it meant she was eating enough to sate her hunger.

The bad news was that her pursuit of the dog was now a game or something more.

What that something might be was still speculation, since none of us knew for certain.

Even so, the increasing length and sharpness of her fangs gave added depth to Tom's polite observation: "With those fangs, she will never need a Halloween costume!"

The adults agreed, though my dad was quick to inquire: "Surely she will need a cape?"

Of course, all we could do was wait and see, while attempting to maintain at least some decorum on those occasions when Julie's sudden presence on our necks was truly unexpected. Hence mom, dad, and I, had to occasionally reenact Tiny's bolting exit.

These momentary escapes did not dampen the humming toddler's enthusiastic pursuit in the least.

MOM, THERE'S A VAMPIRE IN THE HOUSE!

The change all of us were unconsciously expecting occurred on Wednesday, April 27, 2011.

In retrospect, we were disappointed that it had not occurred on April fifteenth, the deadline for filing taxes. That would have been humorously symbolic, but Julie had just turned two, so she was neither aware of, nor concerned about calendars, dates, or taxes.

For her, the operative word was food for while she was not starving, she was not getting what she really needed.

This changed on the twenty seventh, and the first any of us knew about it was when I heard humming unlike anything I had ever heard.

In haste, I raced to the living room, then to the study, and I was so stunned by what I saw that I do not even remember yelling: "Mom!"

The majorly off-key sound of my trembling voice brought mom and dad racing swiftly to where I stood.

What we saw was self explanatory.

Julie had the dog on the floor. Her legs and body weight pinned Tiny's forelegs, leaving her hands free to hold his head down, not that she needed to, because he was not moving a muscle except for small movements here and there.

Equally visible was the fact that Julie's mouth was open wide and her incisors were deep in Tiny's throat.

She was obviously drinking, but we were too stunned to move, yet what we saw was reassuring too, because Tiny seemed to be alright.

He was not in any pain and there was no sign of distress.

No panting or rapid breathing.

No moaning or rolling of the eyes.

Also fostering our inaction was Julie's nonstop humming. It had a soothing trill that was delightfully melodic, though at the time, it seemed blatantly out of place.

In our minds the sound should have been the kind associated with cheap horror films despite the fact that nothing horrifying was happening. She was simply feeding and her humming reflected this, as did the expression on her face.

Her relief and satisfaction was akin to a man who had asthma, who had spent all of his life struggling to breathe, who suddenly finds himself being able to effortlessly breathe in all of the air he needs.

Equally true was that reacting sooner would have changed nothing, for the time between my yell and my parents' arrival was measured in seconds, and seconds later, it ended as Julie gently withdrew her fangs from Tiny's neck.

Sitting up, she looked down at him, patting him in the manner that anyone who has been around a toddler knows well: "Good doggie."

She then looked quietly at us.

What we saw was a face filled with the kind of peaceful relaxation that none of us knew had been absent until this moment.

There was no greed or meanness.

No lust or violence.

No sense of triumph or power.

Just contentment, accompanied by the appearance of increasing vitality which made us realize how incomplete her former diet had been.

Still, none of us knew what to say until mom finally asked: "Julie. Are you hungry?"

"No" and for the first time ever, the finality in her voice was so strong that we understood it perfectly.

She now knew precisely the kind of food she needed, though she did not yet know the word for it.

Then Tiny roused himself.

Leisurely getting up, he walked effortlessly over to his water bowl which was in the kitchen, and he made no effort to flee from Julie. Either then, or later when she walked over and patted him again.

By then, we had sort of recovered.

We now knew that Julie was indeed a vampire and we had absolutely no idea what to do.

Dad was the first to react. Picking up Julie, he lifted her to his shoulder, kissed her cheek, and said: "Julie. Do not hurt Tiny again."

"No hurt Tiny." came the muted protest.

"Feeding on Tiny hurts him."

"No hurt Tiny!" came the more vehement protest.

"Do not bite Tiny."

"Tiny food!"

Dad paused. Suddenly connecting her past words with the present, he asked: "Do I smell like food?"

"No."

"Does mommy smell like food?"

"No."

"What about me?" I needed to know, fearful that the answer might be yes. Dad translated my need into a question: "Does Leo smell like food?"

"No. Eeoo stink."

"Thanks a lot, fang face!"

"Leo!"

"But mom! She said I stink!"

"Well it is time for your bath."

Dad intervened somewhat philosophically: "At least none of us are food. Leo... is your homework done?"

"Most," I admitted noncommittally, refusing to admit even to myself just how much was still left to do.

Even if dad suspected otherwise, he ran with it: "Please take a quick shower. We need to have a family meeting."

31

Mom noted: "We should call the doctors."

Dad agreed: "Please tell them that we need to meet as soon as possible. It should be the four of us. I will take time off from work if needed."

Mom stopped as if splashed by cold water, then reminded him: "We are scheduled to see them tomorrow at seven."

"It would still be best to call and let them know that all of us will be there. Tell them... something unexpected happened... that we need to discuss."

So I took a shower, mom and dad each made phone calls and soon afterwards, the three of us met in the living room.

Tiny was there as well, resting contentedly in his dog bed while Julie occupied herself with a rotating assortment of toys and floor locations. But what each of us noticed the most, was that her giraffe was nearby, yet she was not chomping on its neck the way she always did after a formula feeding.

Mom took a deep awkward breath: "I guess this proves... that she finally got the kind of... food... she needs."

Dad mused: "We now know why she has difficulty closing her mouth when she drinks. Martha... Do you think she can hold out until after we meet with the doctors?"

"We will have to crate Tiny, but she can drink the old stuff until we and doctors figure out something."

I had an idea that I thought was great: "We could get more dogs... or let her take out Bruiser!"

Bruiser was the neighborhood hell-dog on wheels. His owners hated people and liked the fact that their dog terrorized everyone.

Unfortunately, mom laid down the law: "Just because she's a vampire does not mean that she can go around biting whatever she pleases... Gerry? Is something wrong?"

"I was just thinking that she is two... so by the time she turns six or seven she will likely need something bigger than a dog... like a cow... or her feeding might kill it."

"If that is so... then we may have to move because there are only a few cattle left in the southern hills. Most of that pasture land has been turned into grapes."

Dad shook his head in disgust over human values in a world where people were still starving to death: "Wine before cattle!"

Besides, none of us wanted to move because we liked our neighbors more than a lot and Santa Maria suited us just fine.

Shortly before mom and dad married, the assistant manager of the Canoga Park dealership became the manager of the vastly expanded dealership here in Santa Maria.

Because he and dad worked well together and the new dealership needed experienced salesmen, he had invited dad to come work for him and since Santa Maria is between Los Angeles and San Jose where most of mom and dad's families and relatives live, this city was an acceptable midpoint compromise.

Yet even more, on this evening, the moving topic was ignored because dad had a more immediate concern: "We have to be very careful who we talk to and what we say... or all hell will break loose."

He then looked at me: "Telling Tom that Julie is a vampire might cost you his friendship if you do not first explain that she does not consider us to be food. It might be best if we reveal this by inviting Tom and his parents over for a talk."

Since dad said these words instead of mom, I felt the need to defend my friend: "Tom's amazing cool! He's the one who has been saying all along that she is a vampire. Building the coffin was his idea!"

Mom unexpectedly intervened: "Pretending someone is a vampire is one thing. Meeting a real one is another. She scares you... doesn't she?"

"No!" I insisted, defending my bravery, before glancing at my sister and confessing: "Well... a little."

"Well she scares me a little too... so I reckon others will feel the same way. Tom is very special and his parents are too. I would hate to lose their friendship by saying the wrong thing... wouldn't you?"

"Yeah."

Dad muttered: "Now all we have to do is figure out the best way to say it."

At the time, none of us could think of anything and our initial proposals sounded okay while saying them, but afterwards we each wanted our words back because they were so mega-dork.

It was then that Julie tired of her toys and toddled over.

In silence we watched as she walked up to mom, climbed onto her lap, then nestled and hummed in quiet contentment.

Leaning over, dad stroked her head for a moment and mused with a knowing smile: "As far as you are concerned, all is right with the world and you no longer have a care in the world."

As he looked at his daughter, his wife responded: "The world's fine. It's the fanatics and the greedy who make life hell for the rest of us... just like the Book of Revelation says."

She then turned to me: "Leo. You need to finish your homework."

With a nod, I went to my bedroom, wondering what was going to happen, figuring that the worst might be major teasing by the other kids: "Fang Face!" "Where's your coffin?" and things like that.

I also wondered if the horror stories were true and whether I should find a way to lock my bedroom door at night.

For once, I enjoyed doing homework because it distracted me from all of the things I was now preoccupied with.

Things like how Tom and his parents would take the news, or if I should get revenge on the mean girl after whom Julie was named, by revealing to the other kids how my sister had gotten her name.

I then learned that if I really focused on it, the amount of homework I had to do, wasn't as much or as time consuming as I thought, allowing me to go to bed on the early side.

As I picked up Julie and gave her the usual good night hug, she nestled her lips against my throat and I jumped a little.

Since mom noticed my reaction, I attempted to reassert my by bravery: "Julie... are you hungry?"

As I spoke, I tilted my head, exposing my neck.

She in turn, looked at me with the blunt candor only a toddler can muster: "No. Eeoo stink."

MEDICAL DIAGNOSIS: VAMPIRE!

Somehow, I made it through school on Thursday, April 28, 2011, without freaking out, or blabbing like a blubbering idiot.

Tom noticed that something was up, so I told him: "My sister has a doctor's appointment tonight and we all have to be there."

"She's going after Tiny again?"

"Big time..." I mumbled and because I was unable think of anything more to say, I shrugged and changed the subject and that night, Julie wanted the dog again, but mom made her wait: "First we go to the doctor."

Julie angrily refused the formula mom offered, so we got in the car, giving Tiny the run of the house, since taking him with us would have been more than just unwise, given how Julie was eyeing him.

After the exams, Julie did not waste a second: "Want Tiny now!"

Mom reminded her: "Tiny is at home. Do you want food?"

"No! Want Tiny!"

This became the lead-in for dad to tell the doctors what had happened last night, and in the silence that followed, he inquired: "Since she is a vampire and needs to feed on blood, can we arrange to do this in a manner that you can study?"

The doctor overseeing the group, Ryan Allen, DO, an Osteopathic Physician, took a deep breath, then spoke for the others: "First, we need to verify that this claim is true..."

Mom jumped in: "She's hungry! Last night, after feeding on Tiny, she did not want anything more to eat at all. Not even in the morning before going to bed."

Dad offered: "We have no objections to having you come over tonight and seeing for yourselves... how she feeds... or if one you has a big dog you can bring here now?"

Theodore Elam, MD, wanted to know: "What about a cow?"

Dad shrugged: "Good question. She has never been around anything except neighborhood dogs and cats, and after she began playing Chomp Neck, we had to limit the evening social outings we had arranged up till then."

Dr. Susan Galt wanted to know: "How did the dog react to being fed upon?"

Mom took over: "Tiny did not seem to mind. Afterwards, he did not run from her at all. He just lazily stretched... then walked over to his water bowl and drank."

"Did he drink more water than usual?"

"Probably... I mean... we kind of had other things on our minds..."

"Ah...yes... understandable."

After an awkward pause, Jose Ruiz, MD, inquired: "You said that the dog walked over to his bowl. Did you notice anything unusual about his walking... wobbling, weakness, zigzagging, or anything else?"

"No," mom shrugged: "Tiny walked fine except that he no longer limps."

"Tiny had a limp?"

"Yes." Mom blithely noted: "He's nine and a half and has arthritis in his left hip. Our veterinarian recently gave us medication for the pain..."

Suddenly, the implications of what she had just said, caused her to stop, then wonder: "...but since he is no longer limping, maybe I should ask Dr. Thorn to cancel the prescription?"

Dr. Allen immediately called our veterinarian, Dr. Lucile Thorn.

After confirming the arthritis, he suggested that she and the doctors meet at our house tonight, as soon as possible.

By eight thirty, Julie's doctors and our veterinarian were gathered in our living room.

At our request, they brought video cameras which they quickly set up, then dad held Julie while Dr. Lucile Thorn examined Tiny.

The veterinarian shook her head in amazement: "When I examined him back in February, I could feel from his reactions to palpation that his arthritis was far advanced. Earlier X-rays confirmed the extent of it throughout his left hip... but now, he appears to be free from arthritic pain and he is frisker too."

My parents and I agreed and everyone noticed how Julie was eyeing the dog, so dad told her: "Do not hurt Tiny."

"No hurt Tiny," she echoed and as dad set her on her feet, she began humming.

Tiny reacted by starting to move, so Julie froze, but continued humming and the dog yawned, turning his head away, allowing the girl to sneak closer, and the closer she got to him, the more soothing her hum became.

Then with a hum, she pounced, gently rolling him onto the floor and before Tiny could react, she had him pinned and was moving her head, seeking the artery.

Within a second, she found it and angling her head, she opened her mouth wide, then bit and drank.

Awe filled the room as the stunned doctors watched this seemingly surreal event unfolding before their eyes, knowing that it was being recorded, realizing that they were witnessing something that no one but us had ever seen.

When it was over, Julie again patted Tiny, told him he was a good doggie, then she silently snuggled in mom's lap because there were so many people in the room.

As for Tiny, he seemed as unaffected by this feeding as the first one, and he did not mind at all when our veterinarian checked and noted how swiftly the bite wound was healing.

Next, Dr. Thorn poured a measured amount of water into his bowl and offered it to him in the living room, measuring what was left after he finished.

Six ounces was what he drank and as before, he showed no fear when Julie at mom's request, walked over and patted him.

Julie also let the doctors briefly examine her before racing back to the security of the waiting lap.

By then, the doctors had recovered, so dad built on what they knew: "The formulas kept her alive until she could feed. My concern is that too much feeding on one animal will hurt it... and it might be good to learn if she can feed on other animals, like cows and sheep, and if her bites will be as beneficial for them as for Tiny."

After giving them a moment to consider his words, he stated the obvious: "As you know, this kind of experimental feeding is beyond our family resources... and the other issue is how to reveal this information... given how violent American fanatics can be."

There was no need to say more for all of them knew the imaginary self created fears that people have idol-worshiped down through the centuries, and how these could explode if not handled properly.

Fanatics have even deliberately murdered doctors and innocent bystanders in the name of a religion whose founder commanded His followers to never be angry or hate, let alone kill.

Dr. Thorn revealed: "Since I tend a herd south of Orcutt, I have access to cattle. I will know by noon tomorrow if the rancher will allow us to have ongoing access to a cow or two."

Dr. Allen reminded his colleagues: "The Surgeon General's Office is now monitoring our work. They have just begun overseeing all FDA grants to ensure that the corporate favoritism scandals are not repeated.

"I will leave a message tonight and if my hunch is correct, we will likely have visitors from Washington over the coming days... for as Mr. Wynn rightfully noted... the politics of this situation could become dicey if handled wrong. Besides, they will need to modify the grants or write new ones. Even if the only thing her bites do is cure arthritis in dogs, they will want to study this."

As for Julie's feeding needs, these were no longer in doubt.

Video documentation alone, confirmed the benefits she derived from drinking blood and her refusal to drink human blood when Dr. Thorn offered, along with her decree: "You no food," was nice to have for the record.

The other thing we learned thanks to the recordings, was that despite our perceptions to the contrary, Julie's feedings were fast.

Each video recorder had its Time Documentation function on, so calculating the time: One minute, forty seven seconds from bite to withdrawal, was scientifically accurate.

The awareness that we were about to become part of medical and world history whether we wanted to or not, had also been indirectly brought to our attention.

Later that evening after privacy had been restored, dad decreed: "We need to tell family and very close friends... but do not announce it. Let the doctors and the government do that. If anyone asks what is happening, tell them Julie is medically unique and that the doctors are studying her."

Since this was already known to most in the neighborhood, and to those in elementary school who knew me, these words did not cause a ripple, but our phone calls soon did.

When I awakened on the morning of the twenty ninth, my parents shared the news to date.

Tom's parents had agreed to come over tonight.

Phone calls to grandparents and others were pending.

Dad told me: "Like yesterday, any homework you have, get it done before six, because the next few days are going to be locoweed."

When I asked how Julie's night went, mom smiled: "It is so nice not having to guard the dog!"

That was good for a laugh, and a laugh was what I got when Tom asked what tonight's meeting was about.

I quipped by playing it straight: "The doctors have suddenly discovered my sister and they want to study her big time!"

Tom grinned: "Medical diagnosis: Vampire!"

"Yeah! Especially when they learn about her coffin!"

We laughed and left it at that, and when I came home from school, I actually completed my homework and got to be in on a few family phone calls.

As expected, their shock was akin to our own, though mom and dad softened the blow by announcing: "Medically, the doctors now think that Julie might actually be a genuine vampire... but they want to conduct further tests before finalizing their decree and making it public. This means more studies and we will likely be spending part of every evening away from home."

This was the way dad explained it when Tom and his parents, Paul and Susan Gentry came over. Once everyone was seated in the living room, refreshments in hand, mom told them: "We want to share the latest Julie news before it goes public."

Dad then spoke the now well worn explanation without making it sound like an aged recording being replayed as fast as possible.

In the silence that followed, we all looked at each other and I turned to Tom: "You were right all along! You were the one who first thought she was a vampire!"

Tom grinned shyly and since all of the adults were looking at him, he muttered: "It was kind of obvious..." then cautiously, he asked: "What's it like living with a real vampire?"

Since he was looking at me, I answered: "A little spooky... but that's all... cause she does not want our blood... at all. To her, it's not food. The only one who needs to worry is Tiny."

Mom and dad shared all that had happened and by then, it was nearing six thirty. At this time of year, it was dark enough that Julie could come out of her castle since our house was a newer one.

Hence, it was insulated just enough.

She also did not seem surprised to see the Gentry family.

After Julie practiced greeting and wishing us good evening, she wanted to know: "Where is Tiny?"

Dad delivered the news: "In the backyard. Tonight we are going to a ranch, so you can try feeding on a cow."

"No want cow! Want dog!"

Mom knew that Julie did not really know what a cow was, so she explained: "A cow is like a dog... only bigger and better."

"Want Tiny!"

"After the cow!" came the parental duet, whereupon Tom tested the waters: "Do you want a drink?"

His offer, enhanced by the same neck revealing gesture I had made, was soundly rejected: "You no food! Want Tiny!"

Susan grinned: "If Tiny needs a place to hide, please tell us."

Mom was hopeful: "If she likes cows better than dogs, it will make life around the house, a whole lot easier..."

The volcano thundered: "No like cow! Like dog!"

Tom made his views known: "Take out Bruiser and the neighborhood will name the street after you."

I partially missed the bus, so I asked: "Vampire Lane?"

Tom's father, Paul, has a great sense of humor: "It is either that, or Bloodsucker Alley, and I prefer the Lane, thank you!"

Paul is an electronics technician who is so knowledgeable and skilled that he became a BMET, a Bio-Medical Electronic Technician.

A BMET repairs and services medical and hospital electronics and has to be among the best and understand medical stuff too, because a faulty machine can cost a person a limb or their life.

However on this evening, his concerns were personal: "If you need help weathering the storm, please let us know. Unless I am off the mark, you could be in for a hurricane."

Paul had served shipboard in the Navy, so knows real hurricanes from first hand experience. He also knows the foul side of persecution and discrimination because his skin is coal black.

Hence he sometimes still experiences the realities of decimation, diminishing though these are, and Susan knows that evil sting too: "Please do let us know. Unless the world has suddenly changed, the crazies will soon be snorting fire out of both ends."

As mom and dad were expressing their appreciation, the doorbell rang for the medical team had arrived.

In addition to the those who had been here last night, there were several newcomers and the man of the moment was Dr. Wendell Wilson, the Surgeon General of the United States.

This confirmed how big things already were, yet Dr. Wilson was a personable gentleman who sought to put everyone at ease: "Given the initial findings, the President decided that it is better to be fast and accurate, than to delay and have to deal with unnecessary rumors and misunderstandings."

As the introductions came to a close, Dr. Wilson turned to Julie: "...and are you the young lady who just happens to be a vampire?"

Twenty five month old Julie had no intentions of changing her priorities for anyone: "No want vampire! Want dog!"

WHY NOT THAT COW?

The trip to the ranch south of Orcutt was short, for Orcutt and Santa Maria have long been an interlocking mosaic of nondescript houses and streets, giving it the feel of a single city.

Those at the ranch were ready for us. Cameras were set up and some focused upon us when our three van caravan arrived.

Although Tom's parents had declined the invitation to witness this feeding, they had permitted Tom to accompany us, actually me.

We hurriedly exited the vans and positioned ourselves to watch.

Only then did mom unbuckled Julie from her car seat.

Nearby, three cows had been hobbled in a holding pen where lighting had been set up. Stepstools were positioned next to each cow, since Julie was far too short to reach the needed neck and cows do not react kindly to being dumped on their sides.

The way we were standing allowed Julie to see all three cows the moment mom lifted her from the seat.

Her humming squeal of delight documented how completely even the slightest thought of dog had vanished from her mind.

In compliance with the doctors' request, mom set Julie on her feet and the humming toddler raced towards the nearest cow, then she suddenly changed directions, heading for one slightly more distant.

Mom, who was staying close, stopped her daughter and asked: "Why not that cow?"

"Cow stink. Like Eeoo."

Perplexed, mom blurted out: "Leo does not smell like a cow!"

"Cow stink! Like Eeoo!" Julie insisted, then added: "Sick!"

She knew what "sick" meant because everyone had been using it to describe her problems, and I had been sick too, back in January.

Still her use of the word sick to describe me and the cow, confused my parents, but not the veterinarian: "After Julie finishes feeding, I will thoroughly examine that cow and quarantined it, just in case."

Her words focused our attention back upon Julie, whose beeline for the chosen cow was hastened by the fact that the animal did not even attempt to move a muscle.

Like Tiny, the cow seemed to enjoy the vampire's humming.

Because the ground was uneven, the stepstool wobbled, forcing mom to lift and hold Julie, who also needed this support to stand on her tiptoes so she could reach the artery.

Her pulsing hum was deeper and richer than when feeding upon Tiny and she was not the lest bit shy about expressing her appreciation afterwards: "Nice doggie."

"Cow," mom offered mechanically.

"Nice cowie," Julie decreed, patting it as only a toddler would think to do.

By this time, the mood was one of awe for the cow had not objected to the presence of strangers or to being fed upon, and again, the cameras and doctors had seen it all, as had Tom and I.

Tom was the first to make his feelings known: "Spooky cool!"

Since the cameras were on, his words were recorded and he was later credited for markedly popularizing this phrase.

Dr. Wendell Wilson, who was standing with dad, next to us, quietly agreed: "Tom. Your words said it all."

By then, mom and Julie had returned, so dad knelt and ask: "Did you like the cow?"

"Cow good!" Julie's unique hum added depth to this sentiment and since she had not hummed like this after feeding on Tiny, dad inquired: "Better than dog?"

"Cow gooder!"

"Is Tiny still food?"

Julie paused, thinking seriously, then decreed: "Snack!"

Obviously she had no intentions of sparing him or ever again missing a meal, yet given how hungry she must have been for the food she really needed, this viewpoint was decidedly justifiable.

This also thoroughly documented that to her, humans are not food, for despite her intense need for blood, she had never once even attempted to bite us.

Dr. Lucile Thorn then came over: "Julie. Do other cows smell stinky like that cow?"

I mentally thanked the veterinarian for not saying Eeoo, as Julie sniffed the air and announced: "Them."

She pointed to the corral opposite from the cow she had fed upon, where a few of this ranch's cattle were penned.

This caused a mummer and the decision was made to take Julie over to that corral.

From outside of the fence, with father holding her, she pointed to five cows, calling each one stinky, then she told us that the others smelled like food.

As the rancher and his two ranch hands quarantined the five cows, Dr. Thorn commenced her examination with the cow Julie had just fed upon. Her words evoked more murmurs: "The bite has already completely healed and it looks like it will not blemish the hide."

Dad wondered: "More grants?"

Mom concluded: "More cows."

Dr. Wendell Wilson let his assessment be known: "Given the benefits to medical science, the Administration will act decisively on your behalf... though some things will take time to arrange. Dr. Allen has already agreed to serve as the go-between."

Kneeling to Julie's level, Dr. Wilson asked: "What would you like?"

Julie's response was instantaneous: "Vampire."

It took a few moments to decipher the perplexing request. Mom solved it: "She thinks vampire is like dog and cow. She wants to try one."

She then picked up her daughter: "Julie. You are a vampire."

"A girl?"

"A girl and a vampire."

The lighting revealed that Julie was grappling with the idea that she could be more than one thing at the same time.

Connecting the two concepts enabled her to decisively conclude: "Vampire no food."

Mom echoed: "Vampires are not food. People are not food."

Her daughter agreed: "People no food. Smell bad."

"Like Leo?"

"No. Eeoo stink."

"Thanks a lot, fang face!"

Dr. Allen stepped in: "Leo. If Dr. Thorn confirms that the stinky cows are indeed sick, we will need to get you in for a medical check up as soon as possible."

These words silenced everyone and I was not the only one who was wondering what was going to happen next.

THE COW IS OUT OF THE BAG

April 30, 2011, was one of the most important days of my life.

Since it was Saturday, I was not expecting my dad to wake me.

Especially given how early in the morning it was.

His words were swift and to the point: "The doctor just called. All of the cows that Julie said stank, have Undulant Fever... a serious illness which can infect humans. They want you in the hospital immediately... for testing."

As far as I was concerned, this was the most non-cool way to start a day, let alone a weekend, and the only reason I did not snap at my sister during my hasty breakfast was because she was already asleep in her castle.

Dad took me to the hospital at seven thirty and as soon as his parents arrived from Reseda, at around eleven in the morning, he left for work and grandpa Terry stayed with me.

By then, I was in a foul mood because I had been examined forwards, backwards, and inside out.

Two separate blood draws, an hour inside of an MRI scanner, head and chest X-rays, breath samples, and breathing tests, plus several doctor examinations complete with lots of questions, made me better able to appreciate how the rat in Ms. Emmer's sixth grade class felt when being placed in a maze, and otherwise studied.

It turned out that dad's leaving for work was a little premature, since the diagnosis was completed by eleven thirty and the doctors needed to meet with both of my parents as soon as possible.

Twelve noon was when they arrived and all of us were ushered into the long familiar office of Dr. Allen, since he was coordinating my exam due to Julie's involvement.

His words were unexpected: "Leo. Your sister may have just saved your life."

After the long moment needed to recover from the stunning announcement, he asked me: "Did you recently have pneumonia?"

Mom answered: "Low grade pneumonia back in January. Dr. Landis said he was cured."

"He is cured of the pneumonia, but there was some clotting.

"The illness weakened him enough that several blood clots formed in his legs. Several of those clots embolized... which in simplistic terms... means that they have floated through the bloodstream and one of them has made its way to his brain.

"Due to its location, if it is not treated immediately, it could cause the kind of stroke that is permanently disabling and most often fatal."

Before any of us could react, Dr. Allen assured us: "Because it was discovered so early thanks to Julie, we can begin with what in lay terms is called clot busting medication... an anticoagulant.

"If it works, that is all we will need to do.

"If it does not work, then a triangulating laser will hopefully eliminate the need for invasive procedures."

Turning to my parents, he told them: "Because the best drug for children is still in the testing phase... if you agree to its usage, I need both of your signatures on the forms and liability releases.

"The reason for recommending this drug is that it has the fewest side effects and complications. It was also approved long ago in Europe, Canada, Japan, and elsewhere, so extensive testing and monitoring have already been completed.

"The only reason it has not been available in this country is due to the protectionism accorded American pharmaceutical companies and for this drug, that ended when the French pharmaceutical company signed a production agreement with one of ours.

"Finally, I took the liberty of verifying that your medical insurance has approved this medication, which they have because it is far cheaper than invasive surgery."

Signing for this drug was acceptable and mom needed to know: "Is there anything we need to do or avoid?"

Dr. Allen nodded: "No roughhousing, no sports, and no physical education classes, until after the clots have dissolved. Here is the note to give to the school. Fatty foods and junk foods should be minimized or eliminated immediately... and remain so for no less than thirty days after the medication has been stopped.

"We also need Leo to come back in three days, then once a week until the clots are gone. These visits can be scheduled at your convenience so they will not disrupt his schooling or your schedules.

"Leo. If you have a sudden headache that is blindingly painful... or if the world seems to be physically warping... or if you feel numbness... or if your words slur when you speak... or if you cannot raise your arms... or if you feel like you are going to faint... tell your parents or teachers immediately. They will call 911 and we will examine you and likely rush you into surgery.

"It is very unlikely that any of these things will happen... but if they do... telling us immediately could save your life. Just stay close to home for the next few weeks and everything will be fine."

These words did not reassure me at all.

Nor did the fact that the first dose of medicine was delivered via injection.

Still, mom reminded me that this was far better than having a very infectious disease because then, I would have had to stay in bed in a hospital isolation ward for days or weeks.

By then, I was more disgruntled by the fact that I could not get out of doing homework, and that my favorite junk foods would be history for over a month, but as the doctor was handing over the list of taboo foods I could not eat and the yuck foods I would be limited to, grandpa Terry entered the conversation.

His words were those I was not expecting: "Gerry has to work and Martha needs her sleep, but if I can have permission to take Leo into the Recovery Ward where stroke victims are treated, he can see what we are trying to protect him from..."

"...and why he should be grateful that his sister sounded the alarm," mom added knowingly.

This tour was doable and the stroke victims I saw made me realize how lucky I was that I could avoid becoming one.

Especially since one of those in the Recovery Ward was only a few years older than I was.

Seeing them, and what could happen, made it easier to accept the restrictions and the upcoming medical exams and I was thankful that my sister's indirect warning had spared me from this fate.

It also made for quiet days because mom insisted that I take it very easy, limiting me to television, computers, board games, reading, and talk.

Since Tom was home, after his parents were briefed, Tom and I went to his room where I told him what had happened, then confessed: "I feel like they do in those books we read. Weird things keep happening and every chapter is something new."

Tom was awed: "You don't need space aliens or nothing, cause you got your sister!"

After an awkward pause he wanted to know: "Are you going to the ranch tonight?"

"Dr. Allen said I can go as long a I dress warmly and stay quiet and the rancher wants us back so Julie can spot stinky cows.

"At breakfast, mom said that spotting them early saved the rancher a ton of money, so he's given written permission for Julie to feed as often as she needs... and dad said that the doctors and the government are talking about buying the cows.

"They need to test them to see if they are safe to eat after she bites them... and if those who eat the meat will benefit cause of what happened to Tiny."

"Awesome! At lunch, I told dad about the cows cause last night, he had to fix a heart-lung machine that broke. He said that certifying meat started with Kosher and USDA... then came Grass-fed, Free Range, Organic, and Non-GMO... so next will be Vampire Approved, and Certified Vampire Bitten!"

To us, those Vampire labels sounded silly and as we laughed, I added: "By A Non-GMO Vampire!"

That confused Tom a little: "Huh?"

I grinned: "Dad said to never say that Julie is GMO... cause if people think that vampires are Genetically Modified Organisms, they will freak and panic too... major and max! ...and..."

In that moment, Tom and I suddenly realized that freak and panic might mean riot and kill, but I continued: "...and he said that science still cannot do anything that complex even by accident, so she's a..."

"...Non-GMO Vampire!" we chorused, grinning.

Tom asked again: "Are you going tonight?"

"I will unless mom says no. Dad's meeting a man who's buying a car, so mom has to go and if I go, grandma and grandpa can too. Dad said it would be good for them to see it, and all of us think that Tiny needs more time between bites."

"Did she feed on him last night?"

"No. One meal a night is all she needs, though in the evening she wakes up on the hungry side."

"Doesn't it bother you that she's hungry?"

"No," I said as we chimed: "Eeoo stink!"

We laughed again and I asked: "Want to come?"

Tom paused, then shook his head, so I asked: "Still spooks you?"

After a longer pause, he admitted: "A little..."

I agreed: "Me too, and maybe more than a little," so we changed the subject and that night I went.

This time there were far more cows and more people and cameras too, which did not bother Julie at all.

Nor was she bothered by the cool damp air and the cutting wind that made the rest of us long for warmer clothing despite being bundled to the max.

That is, all of us except Julie.

Over the past two months, she had been resisting jackets and sweaters to the point where mom had given up trying to get her to wear them, and this was the accidental test because it was unseasonably cold.

The fact that she had insisted upon and dressed in the T-shirt and summer weight pants, revealed that there was no additional clothing underneath, and she had been swift to potty train, thus she had not worn diapers in months.

The end result was a seemingly underdressed girl who did not notice the bitter cold at all.

All she wanted to do was to feed, and the wide platforms next to the four cows hobbled for her, was something she accepted as being the way things were supposed to be, not realizing that they had been built today just for her.

Next grandpa Terry carried her over to the corral.

Of the over five hundred cows, she pointed out fifty seven who stank, and to her, five of those stinkers "smelled different."

It turned out that all of them needed veterinary care.

Most were in the earliest stages of Brucellosis (Undulant Fever).

The five whose stenches were different had problems ranging from Diarrhea, Bloat, and a Puncture Wound, to Mange and Ringworm.

All were easily treated and Tiny got another bite free night, the rancher was very grateful, and the doctors and researchers were having a field day because Julie was genuine.

A vampire who could repeat her successes.

A subject they could study.

The only problem was that rumors were already spreading that something was happening, possibly in Santa Maria, possibly top secret because the President's Press Secretary was evading the topic: "I do not yet know enough to comment. Next question please."

We will probably never know who contacted the news media, but on Sunday, May first, as we headed to the unmarked van that the government was using to drive us to the ranch, two reporters, one wielding a video camera, attempted to question dad.

The driver intercepted them, told them that we were in a hurry, then swiftly ushered us into the van.

As soon as we were buckled in, we drove off, but neither of my parents had any illusions.

Nor did the driver of the van who noted: "They are tailing us."

This was when we learned that those driving these vans were FBI special agents who had come to Santa Maria with the Surgeon General, then been assigned to guard and drive us, and to guard the ranch, for reasons they did not know and did not want to know.

What the agent did was send a coded message via cell phone and change the route.

A short time later, those tailing us had been thwarted enough that the privacy of the ranch was still secure.

Of course, this ultimately changed nothing, forcing Dr. Allen to confess: "The cat is out of the bag."

Julie, who had fed and just finished pointed out the only stinky cow amidst those in the corral, was too young to even know that this was an idiom, let alone what it meant. But as she lounged in mom's arms, she proudly corrected him: "No cat. Cow!"

Actually dear sister, it was you.

REALLY STINKY COWS

On Monday May 2, 2011, the Administration began hinting about Julie's existence.

Their news release stated: "A child was born in Santa Maria in 2009, who has very unique genetics that are now being studied."

Also stated was that the benefits to science, agriculture, and medicine, were potentially immense, but that protecting the privacy of the entire family was mandatory due to: "This child's very unique and unusual needs."

A formal statement was then issued, requesting that the news media not pursue this story.

The words "arrest" and "lawsuits" were not mentioned, but the statement: "If necessary, this Administration will intervene to protect the rights and privacy of this family and their child. The loss of valuable information, or harm to either the family or their child, will be dealt with accordingly," delivered the message.

Unfortunately, those who needed to hear this message were the local reporters who had begun unobtrusively interviewing our neighbors on Sunday the first.

One was the television news team who had informally attempted to interview dad yesterday evening.

The other was a newspaper reporter.

Their Monday morning interview lists, each made independent of the other, later revealed that the Gentry and Wynn families were among those whom each planned to "formally contact" on Monday.

The television team was unaware of the Administration's request when they knocked on the Gentry's door.

Paul, whose current schedule gave him Mondays off, answered the door, and acknowledged their credentials.

He then told them: "I advise you to contact your newsroom immediately. The President's Administration has just issued a major news statement that you need to review to ensure that no federal laws are violated... before continuing or making public, your current investigations. I am sorry, but due to this federal mandate, I cannot be of further assistance to you at this time. Thank you."

Had the reporters heeded his words, all would have been well, but they did not. Instead, they headed to the other end of the block and came knocking on our door, or more correctly, they tried to.

As they walked up to our front door, two of the FBI agents who were covertly guarding us, intercepted them.

By then, Paul had called and told mom what he had told them.

Since dad was at the dealership, mom gave Paul the contact number we had been given and he called what turned out to be a direct line to the FBI.

The response was swift and decisive.

A second FBI team arrived within minutes and politely requested that the reporters accompany them to their television newsroom or risk finding themselves in court facing criminal charges.

The reporters complied and in a private meeting with the FBI and their newsroom supervisor they listened to the Administration's news release and agreed to comply.

Besides, there was a major news story that genuinely needed their immediate attention, but the damage had been done because unbeknownst to those protecting us, Max Smillet, a newspaper reporter, was also trying to unearth what was happening.

By chance, Max had stumbled upon his television counterparts and during the past half hour, he had been tailing them to see if they might be scrounging up leads he had not.

Thus he observed the polite Gentry response and been too far away to hear it, but he then saw the television reporters head straight to our house, where they were stopped by two men who had been sitting in an unmarked car.

A short time later, another unmarked car pulled up and after flashing what from a distance looked like badges, the reporters and newcomers left as a group, unaware that the newspaper reporter had covertly photographed them.

On a whim, Max had driven to the local television studio and photographed the FBI's car and the news van which happened to have been parked next to each other, after which he headed to his office, where he met with his supervisor and learned about the cease and desist request.

This nixed the original story, but minutes later, inspiration struck.

Max went back to his supervisor and offered: "I can put the facts together in an unrevealing manner that could be loads of fun and maybe make a good headline. I can use the facts to document this storyline and no one is going to complain because it will make no attempt to reveal anything about the family or the child."

Due to slumping newspaper sales, Max's supervisor decreed: "Play with it. If it is worth anything, we'll give it a go, but dust off the Miller Street construction scandal, in case we need a filler."

So Max updated the scandal story, then conducted several additional interviews in our neighborhood.

He also made copies of everything, including his photographs, before hiding the originals so they could not be confiscated.

His hope was that these might someday be worth something if they were historically meaningful, which they actually were.

Next, he let the facts conjure up the story and it was so offbeat and eye-catching that the newspaper ran with it.

At the time, we had no idea what was coming.

Thanks to Paul's phone call and what the FBI soon told us, we knew about the thwarted television reporters, but none of us knew about Max Smillet.

Since physical activities were no goes, I had done most of my homework, so was free to join my grandparents Brenna and Brandon Lee, who had come down from San Jose, California, to watch the feeding and learn what had happened.

Since dad was not scheduled to be in the showroom, he decided to go, as did the Gentry family, for Tom had begged them to come.

This was when Jean and Terry Wynn decided to come too.

This meant that a second van was needed which was acceptable since keeping our doings secret by driving our own cars was not a practical option.

The FBI wanted to maintain their security and screening everyone at our house, then driving us, was easier than dealing with a changing group of visitors and cars. Besides, these agents would know when they were being followed. We would not.

For them, this made guarding us and the ranch easier, given the limited manpower they currently had, for bringing in too many agents too fast, would have been revealing in the wrong kind of way.

It saved gasoline too, so all gathered at our house and waited for Julie to awaken from day sleep.

While we waited, talk focused upon all that had happened to date and Paul shared an insight none of us had thought of.

In some parts of the world, the announcement that United States had a vampire might destabilize their pro-American regimes: "Given the brutal realities of European colonization... and the viciousness with which modern western corporations are abusing and plundering what they derogatorily call: Third World Countries... the fact that Julie is white... might be viewed as fitting in an adverse manner. This could then be used to rile up anti-American sentiments... religious or otherwise."

Dad confessed: "I knew there was a reason I never wanted into politics."

He would have said more, but Julie made her grand entrance: "No want dog! Want cow!"

Dad smiled: "Tiny will love that!" He then shepherded Julie through the greeting courtesies as Susan Gentry remarked: "This certainly gives new meaning to the words: Eating out and fast food."

Mom looked somewhat frustrated: "This may force us to move closer to the ranch." She then confessed: "I don't want to move."

Susan, who worked for the city, suggested: "Once your story goes public, if you or the government petitions the city for a zoning change, that would allow you to keep a couple of cows in the backyard."

Grandma Brenna mused: "Since this kind of feeding could be deemed a medical necessity, medical insurance might be required to help defray some of the costs, further mandating the zoning change. You know... it would be fun seeing how the insurance industry reacts to having cows deemed a medical necessity."

Grandpa Brandon built upon her words: "The first battle would be over whether any cow would do... or if they have to be certified as organic and non-GMO."

Julie made her views known: "Want cow now!"

This time, no cars followed us and the mood at the ranch was more laid back because for most of us, this was another repeat.

The only changes were camera angles and the addition of several hand held video recorders.

Julie was more than happy with the good cowie and only five stinkers were found, but these cows were noteworthy because Julie announced: "Cow stink more," as she pointed to each of them.

That same evening, veterinary testing revealed that they had Leptospirosis, mandating inoculations for all herd animals in the region and beyond.

The contagiousness of this bacterial disease and the fact that it can infect humans, made everyone grateful for the timely warning.

Thus yet again, Julie was the hero of the moment though she was naturally unaware of this.

When we got home, she was contented enough to put up with a brief medical examination which confirmed that she had gained more weight and grown more during the past six days than she had during the previous two months.

This was the ultimate confirmation that she was a vampire and that for better or worse, the world would never be the same.

NECKS YOU HAVE TO CATCH

For us, the changes began after the May second feeding.

We were accompanied home by Dr. Ryan Allen and five government officials who had just witnessed Julie's feeding and herd assessment, but they were not introduced until after all of us had recovered from yet another damp windy evening.

That is all except Julie, who had not been the least bit cold.

The time was also spent helping first time witnesses through their emotions and thoughts.

Paul Gentry was the first to speak. Turning to his son, he confessed: "You were very right, Tom. We needed to see this. It enables us to better understand the complexities of the situation."

In response, Dr. Allen asked if the Gentry family's participation in the upcoming meeting was acceptable to all.

Since it was, they stayed, which I appreciated because having someone my own age in these meetings meant much to me.

Next, Susan admitted that talking things over afterwards was a good way to recover from the realization that God's plan for creation is larger than mankind.

Grandma Jean jumped in: "And it includes women too!"

After Amens all around and once everyone was ready, Dr. Allen introduced the representatives from the Department Of the Interior (DOI), the Food and Drug Administration (FDA), Agriculture (USDA), Health and Human Services (HHS), and Education (Dept. of Ed.).

He concluded: "They are not ranked high enough to attract general news media attention, yet each of them answers directly to the Cabinet Secretaries of their respective agencies."

By prior agreement, Ms. Ewing from the DOI, spoke for the group: "The Administration sent us because there are multiple concerns that need to be swiftly addressed. From family and personal needs, to agricultural and medical research... to determining the best way to manage the revelation of Julie's existence... since the pot is boiling and we cannot keep the lid down much longer."

Mom began by revisiting her ongoing concern: "If at all possible, we would like stay here. The neighbors are great and the location is ideal. Gerry has an excellent relationship with his coworkers in the dealership and his seniority and customer contacts are the reason I can be a full time mom until Julie is old enough to go to daycare..."

Mom paused, belatedly realizing that Julie would likely not be attending daycare, so returning to her former job as a bookkeeper might not be as easy as it had been when I was younger.

However, it was grandma Brenna who moved things along: "How is the castle protecting her?"

This required an explanation and Julie got to show off her castle.

Upon returning to the living room, dad shared a concern: "If she becomes more sensitive to sunlight, she will need more granite to protect her." He then half jokingly announced: "Castles are next to nil in this city and even fewer have basements."

Dr. Atherton from the HHS noted: "NASA, the Department of Defense, and others are working to perfect insulating materials, so arranging tests will be easy and scientifically revealing. These materials could potentially meet Julie's shelter needs in a manner that might allow her to live inside of houses and even travel."

I sighed and Tom grinned: "Leo would rather have the castle."

Paul noted: "A castle might end up being necessary depending upon how the fanatics and fear mongers react."

Susan built upon his words: "Those kind of reactions could adversely impact her socialization needs."

This further validated her husband's decree of complexity, since socialization would in some ways be more important than education.

Even if Julie only learned to read, write, and do basic math, she would still be able to earn a very good living by spotting sick cattle and other animals and sick people too, before the actual onset of their illnesses. But if she did not know how to interact with her peers and with people in general, that could have unwanted and even tragic consequences.

Dad provided indirect proof by detailing the current Chomp Neck dilemma because Julie still enjoyed playing it, albeit without the bite, but to her, a neck was a neck, so all were fair game despite parental attempts to limit necks to stuffed animals.

This, along with Julie's sensitivity to sunlight, was limiting play with her peers to tightly supervised early evening outings, allowing Ms. Eider from the Department of Education to state: "Special Education or other funding, will likely be needed to meet her educational needs since she cannot attend regular day classes. I will add this need to the list."

Then came the most intriguing of the personal issues.

Feeding.

For now, Dr. Lu from the FDA confirmed that this agency and the USDA wanted to restrict Julie's feedings to the ranch's cattle, though having her check nearby herds would be more than just for the sake of research, for the moment other ranchers learned what she could do, they would be demanding the right to have her services.

This implied the need to set up a system so Julie could do the work and get paid for it, and because this service was valuable, the government did not want anyone taking advantage of her or us.

The USDA's Ms. Llewellyn added that restricting her feedings to just the ranch would allow the USDA and the FDA to conduct tests on the cattle to determine what her bites were doing and whether the meat would remain fit for human consumption.

Equally valid was the need to see if her bites would benefit other animals the way they had Tiny, and even more needful was to learn what the long term effects might be.

Would her bites cure arthritis, but cause cancer or something else?

No one yet knew and these questions needed to be answered.

Next came the issue of public revelation and Paul's concerns about world reactions were acknowledged as being a major concern.

Equally a concern were the public's fears regarding GMOs.

Then there was the issue of America's homegrown fanatics.

To show how serious the last concern was, Ms. Ewing revealed that plans were already in the works to permanently increase security at the hospital due to genuine fears that some lunatic or fanatic would bomb it solely because Julie just happened to have been born there.

This implied that the same level of protection might be mandatory for us and our neighbors, if we decided to stay.

As for problem neighbors, the only ones any of us could think of were those around the corner who owned the dog, Bruiser, because they hated everyone anyway.

Finally, we focused upon finding the best way to reveal Julie to the world and a lot of ideas were proposed, some in jest, including a Halloween Coming Out Party.

In the end, our proposal was to reveal the economic and scientific benefits.

Next would come limitations like being unable to eat the kinds of foods we do and sunlight issues.

This would be followed by pictures and videos of Julie and us being family, before telling the history of events and announcing that she is a vampire.

It was a good plan and this format was adopted, but that came after the cow was part way out of the bag because the world had other plans.

So too did my sister, as dad learned the hard way when Julie's sudden humming appearance on his neck caught all of us by surprise, inadvertently documenting how good this twenty five month old girl already was, when it came to playing Chomp Neck.

In the aftermath of that meeting disrupting moment, dad reminded her: "Julie! No Chomp Neck on people! No Chomp Neck on mommy. No Chomp Neck on Leo. No Chomp Neck on daddy. Chomp Neck only on your stuffed animals."

"Chomp Neck only on Spot and Brownie," mom echoed, referring to Julie's giant stuffed giraffe and horse.

"No! Gooder!"

None of us could initially decipher what she meant, so I asked: "Like cow?"

She thought for a moment, then decreed: "No cow. Play."

Tom teased: "Like Leo?"

"No," came the predictable retort: "Eeoo stink."

This was when Ms. Eider, who has a Ph.D. in child psychology, mused: "What you probably want is a neck you have to catch."

Julie smiled as she gleefully linked this word to her favorite game: "Catch neck!"

This drove home to all of us, for the first time, that this girl's focus and priorities were totally and completely those of a vampire.

THE GMO PANIC OF 2011

My dad is probably in the minority in that he reads newspapers from cover to cover everyday, even today.

He enjoys it, but for him, it was work related since he had to be ready to note, discuss, or comment upon any local or national story, and of course, sports, entertainment, and the weather.

The weekly auto section with its autos wanted, auto sales, and dealer advertising, were professionally useful.

However the May 3, 2011, Tuesday edition of Santa Maria's local newspaper ran a secondary story on its front page.

Its headline riveted his attention.

Children Believe A Vampire Lives In East Santa Maria
Did escorting TV reporters from this
area erroneously confirm their belief?

Max Smillet's story was never meant to be serious.

Nor did it proclaim that a vampire even existed.

It read: "In spite of the fact that Halloween is months away, some children on the east side of Santa Maria believe that a vampire is living in their neighborhood.

"A number of children, when questioned individually over the past several days, have told this reporter their belief that there is a child who reportedly sleeps during the day, inside of a castle located in the garage of their family's home, then supposedly awakens after sunset and prowls the night.

"The fact that television news reporters were escorted from their neighborhood was considered by some of these children to be proof that the recent Administration announcement is really an attempt to keep this vampire hidden from public view.

"When asked why the government would do such a thing, the children's answers ranged from 'They want it to be a secret' to 'It's a secret weapon' to fight crime, or terrorists, or space aliens, or pollution, or global warming, or monsters, including other vampires.

"One very bright six year old girl decreed 'They created it so children have to behave in school.'

"When asked what makes them think that a vampire is roaming the streets at night, the children's answers include spooky sounds, reports of missing family pets, and classmates who refuse to reveal secrets about the castle in the garage or the mysterious home wherein the castle is said to be.

"These non cooperative classmates mostly insist that there is no such castle. Typical comebacks include 'Who would want to put a castle in a garage?' 'What castle?' and 'Get real!'

"Actual sightings of the vampire are totally nonexistent for the children admit to having never seen it, but dark shadows are enough to satisfy childhood needs to see whatever justifies the belief.

"At least when talking with other children, who all agree that spooky shadows would be the perfect place for a vampire to hide.

"The spookier the shadow, the better!

"They also insist that a coffin would not be a good place for a vampire to hide since everyone knows that vampires hide in them.

"The parents of these children are convinced that there is no truth to the vampire rumor, any more than there was to the recent werewolf tale that has long since vanished like a neglected ghost.

"Still, a few parents admit that they have heard that there is a house which has a stone structure nicknamed 'the castle.'

"This newspaper refuses to pursue stories of that kind, in deference to Administration requests to respect the privacy of the unnamed child and family mentioned in its news release, since these kind of stories might accidentally reveal harmful information.

"What can be said is that the unique blending of incomplete facts, along with rumors and imagination, has created a modern day myth.

"Hence the coincidental escorted departure of television news reporters from this area might have unwittingly encouraged an obvious childhood fantasy. That is, from a child's perspective.

"This points to the need for extra awareness on the part of the public and guidance from parents, so that rumors and speculations do not create harmful falsehoods or lead to inadvertent revelations that could be damaging."

By itself, this story would have been completely harmless and potentially very helpful. However, as Susan Gentry later remarked: "Too many people knew just enough to add small pieces of wood to the growing gossip pile and it suddenly became a bonfire."

Actually, the headline was problematic because more people scanned the headline, than read the story.

This edition of the newspaper also sold more copies than usual, so more people saw it.

What happened was that those who did not read the story, along with those who incompletely read the headline, and those who imperfectly remembered it, all assumed that it was about the vampire, rather than about childhood beliefs and the need for adult guidance.

Also everyone knows that newspapers do not print news stories unless they have the documentation to protect themselves from lawsuits, so the instant assumption was that this story was fact based proof that a vampire existed.

Therefore, many people assumed that the Administration was indeed trying to hide it and therein lay the real concern: Why would the government need to hide this vampire's existence?

This concern heightened tensions and created more rumors that grew as more information and speculations were added.

The adults whose kids came over to play with Julie or with me, knew about the castle.

Others had seen it, or heard of it being built.

More than a few adults and children knew that Julie was a night owl, and that she had physical problems which made normal feeding difficult and that she had not been expected to live.

The reason they knew this, was because mom and dad and I did not blab about such things, but we did not keep them secret either.

The only reason Tom and I and our friends, did not talk about the castle when asked, was because we did not want to get laughed at.

We mostly changed the subject and talked about other things.

Of course the recent nightly visits to our home and our trips from it had been noticed, while reports of "things happening" on a cattle ranch south of Orcutt during the time we were away from home, fueled speculations whenever this tidbit crossed paths with our doings.

Apparently, the bright lights used to film Julie had been noticed.

Thus the rumors grew and spread.

On May fourth, the newspaper and its reporter admitted in a front page editorial, that the "Vampire Belief Report" was acceptable, but that its headline and timing "had been a lapse in judgment, since it indirectly helped bring into being, the speculations and unfounded rumors that were never the intent of this newspaper or that article."

That same day, the television reporters stated in their news broadcasts and later in print: "We were aware of the childhood beliefs, but that was not the story we were working on when we were summoned to the newsroom to investigate and cover the sudden change in the State's water allocation to Santa Maria's farmers. This decrease obviously was and is still major news."

These newspaper and television denials did nothing to dampen the rumors and all in the know were in a moral bind, because Julie is indeed and in fact, a vampire and she was sleeping in our garage in a stone room called: the castle.

On the other hand, she had only just turned two, so she was most certainly not wandering the streets at night.

Still, had this been the extent of the rumors, or if they had been limited to Santa Maria, nothing would have likely happened.

The problem was that Santa Maria was on national and international radar screens because the Administration's remarks had been broadcast worldwide and posted on the internet.

In response, many millions of people sought more information.

Thus the local newspaper's internet edition and its "Children Believe A Vampire" headline received so many hits that it crashed the system, yet still managed to spread throughout the nation and around the world.

So did many internet variants on the local rumors and soon, a few believers in the occult and the supernatural, but mostly fanatics who had long believed that the coming of the antichrist would be accompanied by legions of demonic inhuman monsters, began decreeing that this story was: "A covert attempt to sound the alarm and reveal the actual existence of a real vampire."

They reacted as if a "demonic vampire" really existed.

Most held special meetings and prayer vigils and survivalist equipment and weapons sales reached an all time high.

The sale of garlic and silver also shot through the roof.

A few believers also proclaimed their intent to go to Santa Maria.

Some openly wanted to see and admire the creature.

Others professed their intent to: "Kill the monster before it spawns," and "The family of the monster" was deemed "a legitimate target."

However, at the time, this was the small stuff.

So small, that what concurrently happened, thwarted most of the adore or kill the monster pilgrimages, and majorly delayed the rest.

The real issue was that billions of people genuinely believed that governments were hiding the truth.

They believed that Genetically Modified Organisms had changed the unnamed child into a monster and that governments and the corporations that controlled those governments, did not want to reveal that "a GMO transformation was what had actually happened."

These people believed that the only reason the unnamed Santa Maria child had even been mentioned, was because the United States had no choice because "too many people already knew about the monster child's existence."

Therefore, the government had to reveal it or lose credibility.

These fears were enhanced by confirmation that Santa Maria was surrounded by farmland and by Santa Maria's ranking as the fifth windiest city in the nation.

In turn, these facts became the basis for "rumors that Santa Maria's farmers grew GMO crops" and thanks to the wind, these imaginary stories gave rise to even more rumors and speculations because the source of these fears was too close to home.

The public knew that Genetically Modified Organisms were real.

Equally known was that the corporations had demanded that governments not regulate GMOs in any manner.

Equally known was that the corporations had rigged the laws so that no GMO studies or research were mandated, nor was safety testing required.

Just as well known was that all of this was being done solely for the sake of corporate profits.

To this same end, the other intent was to eliminate the issue of corporate liability by utilizing the excuse: "No testing was ever required by the government, so we had no way of knowing…"

Hence the public's fearful belief was that whatever GMOs had transformed the child into a monster, had long ago been carried by the winds to other parts of the country and the world.

There were also fears regarding what those supposedly poisonous GMOs would do to children and adults.

These fearful beliefs spread like wildfire, producing terror and panic not seen since the infamous "War of the Worlds" radio broadcast of October 30, 1938, when the fictional story of Martians invading the Earth, was mistakenly thought to be real.

Moreover, since GMOs had never been regulated or tested, and no safeguards had been put in place or imposed, there were no genuine or meaningful ways to squelch these fears.

Especially since the bulk of the public no longer trusted the corporately owned news media.

Nor did they trust the corporations to tell the truth.

The May fifth response was an economic disaster.

Foods that were not genuinely certified as 100% Organic, or 100% Non-GMO, languished on the shelves because most people were not willing to risk eating them.

Many government labels including USDA Organic, also languished since these rightly did not contain the words 100% Organic.

Hence more than a few people now feared that these foods were only partly organic and that they were being "deliberately labeled as Organic" to dupe people into eating "GMO laced Stealth Foods."

Others simply no longer trusted government labels.

In desperation, unlabeled foods and those that were solely government labeled, were removed from the shelves by store owners who did not want their stores vandalized or burned down by those trying to rid the world of this perceived source of danger.

Meanwhile, people who were not farmers, banded together and headed into the countryside where they burned fields suspected of being non-organic.

In their ignorance, more than a few organic farms were burned.

Corporate food processing plants, chemical companies, seed storage companies, and more, became the targets of arson and vandalism. So too were truck and train grain haulers suspected of having carried the supposedly deadly organisms.

By May sixth, martial law had been declared almost worldwide and in the United States, the National Guard was called out.

Thankfully, order was restored before too much physical damage was done, but the economic losses were immense, worldwide and in the United States.

Later calculations verified that GMO regulations and safety testing would have cost around ten to twenty million dollars.

The economic losses from people's fears of GMOs, their absolute refusal to eat them, and their intense desire to forever rid the world of them, resulted in over five trillion dollars in financial losses to the food industry alone.

These losses severely impacted other industries too, so in an effort to save the economy, minimize the damage, and prevent mass public uprisings, the United States government felt that it had no choice but to fully reveal Julie's existence sooner rather than later.

My parents naturally gave their permission.

Especially after mom concluded that the stars and numbers also mandated it.

Saturday afternoon on May seventh, the Administration announced that martial law would remain in effect until May fourteenth, and that public schools would be extended an extra week to make up for the lost days.

In the same breath, they announced that GMO regulations and mandatory safety testing laws, and genuine organic certification and confirmation laws, had been sent to Congress.

Finally, they were going to begin revealing "everything" related to the Santa Maria child starting tomorrow: "The only reason for not revealing it today... is because too many people do not want to listen. They want to be scared. They want to be fearful... but what they really want, is an excuse to kill and destroy.

"They want us to legitimize their terrorism.

"Therefore, we will not give them this excuse... or any other.

"Until this insanity passes. Until common sense and the ability to listen has been restored, information will be slowly and carefully released so as not to give those vile fear mongering terrorists the excuses they want and need."

The first tidbits were released on May 8, 2011, when the FDA, the Food and Drug Administration, spoke about the scientific benefits the unusual child could potentially provide in a manner that science and technology could one day duplicate.

From the ability to detect sickness in people and animals before it becomes serious, to finding cures for illnesses like arthritis.

Also proclaimed was that this research would take years because no one wanted a repeat of the GMO panic.

Since polls showed that this news was positively received, on the ninth came the Surgeon General's statements regarding the unnamed child's intolerance to sunlight, backed up by documented human illnesses and genetic disorders that doctors have known about for centuries.

These illnesses and genetic disorders make sunlight unbearable or dangerous for those afflicted, and this same level of detail was provided to document feeding restrictions, but the only specific issue noted was that the unique child could only drink fluids.

Tuesday, May tenth, was the day family, medical, and government, videos and photos were broadcast while a running commentary was provided. The only name released on this day was: "Julie who lives with her family in Santa Maria."

Pictures included mom holding Julie when she was a newborn, family baby videos, Julie playing with her toys, but only two were shown where she was sucking on them.

One was the typical absentminded leg chew, for at that age, she had no idea what she was chomping on and everything went into the mouth. The other was a neck bite and the expression on her face confirmed that she was just sucking on it because it was there.

Also shown were the medical videos of Julie's heartrending struggle to drink liquid formulas, and one mom made that showed Julie seeking shade under her crib, pressing herself against the wall.

These were followed by a video dad made which just happened to show Tiny limping in obvious pain, while ten month old Julie crawled past him.

The final sequences began with Julie pointing out cows that did not look sick at all, followed by veterinarians talking about her successful identification of those highly infectious animals before they could spread their diseases to other cattle and to humans.

Next came a USDA inspector who documented how much money Julie had saved ranchers and consumers thanks to her timely warnings.

Last were the recent videos showing Tiny no longer limping, mixed with the one showing him limping, as an FDA official revealed: "Veterinarians and doctors have documented that thanks to Julie, this dog no longer suffers even the slightest pain despite the fact that he still has severe arthritis.

"Research is now underway to determine how Julie did this so we can one day make drugs that will hopefully be as successful in treating arthritis and similar diseases in humans and animals."

This presentation was well received and commentators were lighting fast to proclaim: "The accuracy of the Administration's claims have been confirmed beyond any doubt. Julie obviously has unusual medical needs, yet the study of her unique abilities can potentially be of tremendous benefit to science, agriculture, and medicine.

"This explains the Administration's concerns regarding the loss of valuable information, and their concerns for the child's safety.

"In turn, this documents that the Administration's reasons for prolonging confidentiality were for the sake of the child, and for the sake of the research that will hopefully one day benefit us all."

At our house, the expected came in the form of instant recognition.

Ongoing phone calls and knocks on our door kept us preoccupied, for the FBI would only reveal themselves if there was an obvious problem, or if we summoned them.

Their assistance was thankfully not needed, though my parents had to minimize prying by repeating parrot-like: "The government has requested that they be the only ones to release this information. Given the crisis caused by the GMO panic, do we want to risk a repeat?"

This wording and my version of it were suggested by Dr. Allen when he briefed us: "Say more than this and you might wish that you had been born without a mouth."

Therefore, I told the kids: "If I say anything, we will be skinned alive by our parents, then by the police!"

"Non true!"

"No! Max true! That's why the police told mom and dad to write down the names of everyone who visits us, including you."

Showing them the list took the pressure off, but this did not stop me from worrying about tomorrow when our names would go worldwide. Neither Tom nor I knew what to say about the upcoming revelation, or the GMO panic, or martial law.

The fact that school had been suspended for a week was cool.

The additional week in June was not.

Tom looked absently out of the window of his room where I had taken temporary refuge: "Dad thinks they are doing things right, but that this will not stop the crazies or the fanatics."

I noted: "Mom said if it slows them down, that should be enough. Dad thinks the real problem is that some people might still panic and that your dad is max right. The foreign response could be major bad."

Tom agreed, then asked: "You going to the feeding tonight?"

"No. Dad is staying home because friends and family will be calling, and when you've seen one stinky cow, you've seen 'em all."

"Yeah. You scared about the interview?"

Tom was referring to the interview that would be recorded this evening for airing either tomorrow or soon thereafter.

I shrugged: "I don't know," which was true because cameras had been present since the night the doctors had recorded Julie's feeding, and I was kind of wishing that they and all of the other people would just go away so I could have my normal life back.

I also felt like I no longer knew what normal was supposed to be.

As Susan Gentry later phrased it: "When you have a vampire in the house, normal takes on a whole new meaning."

THE ULTIMATE QUESTION

That night, we were interviewed, then mom took Julie out for what my parents now called: "Her nightly cow."

Given the number of visitors and nonstop phone calls, dad was more than grateful when he was finally able to crawl into bed, while the fact that my grandparents had chosen to return and be with us now that we were about to be formally revealed, was reassuring.

The presence of several close relatives was deeply appreciated, and all there helped with the phone calls and emails.

For us, the fateful time was nine in the morning, Pacific Time, on May 11, 2011, because the government wanted daylight to rule the sky should panic occur.

This timing also prevented the fanatics from proclaiming that the revelation was being made at night in deference to Satan.

It began with the Administration Press Secretary's announcement that after the news briefing, an uncut, unedited interview with the family of Julie would be aired in full.

She then introduced Surgeon General Wendell Wilson, MD, who gave parental names and told the history from the medical side, complete with photos, explanations, and extensive documentation that GMOs had played no part at all, in Julie's creation.

Next came the fateful words: "According to medical science, Julie Wynn is biologically classified as a vampire of human origins... because her parents are fully human and Julie's DNA is fully human too... albeit in a manner that will take Geneticists decades of study to understand and explain... for as I have just documented... we have absolutely ruled out even indirect or inadvertent GMO contamination or interference in Julie's genetics.

"Again, I will remind you that there are no GMOs anywhere in her body, in her blood, or in her genetic structure.

"None at all.

"This is precisely why unraveling the mystery of how she came to be created solely from human genetics is such a complex and complicated endeavor. One that will reveal a wealth of information once it has finally been fully and completely deciphered.

"To me, this is the ultimate proof that God can create anything, any time, in a manner that proves His perfection and His wisdom... because from the medical standpoint, she a perfect creation in that her body has no flaws... like having the correct teeth, but the wrong stomach or a weak heart... and just as revealing is that she was created to feed solely upon only one kind of blood.

"Animal blood and only animal blood.

"She totally refuses to drink human blood even when it is offered to her. We have also thoroughly documented that even when she was painfully starving because no one suspected that she needed animal blood... she never made even one single attempt to bite or feed off of her parents or any other person.

"Never. Not even once.

"Since God has blessed her with a uniquely keen sense of smell and the ability to communicate, we will one day be able to test her sense of smell in a manner that will enable us... with the technology we currently have... to create machines that do what she can already do. To smell in human and animal scents, the existence of illness before it becomes contagious or untreatable.

"This can do more than just save millions of lives worldwide.

"It has the potential to eliminate the suffering that comes from being afflicted with a disease that is untreatable in its later stages.

"This alone, might one day lead to the elimination of all illnesses.

"Finally, the only concerns we have, are those that will take time and scientific testing to unravel.

"The first is meat safety in regards to cattle or any other livestock that Julie feeds upon.

"Therefore, thorough testing is being done and will be completed before any animal Julie feeds on, will be made available in the market place. However, even if safety is totally confirmed and even if the medical benefits of eating vampire bitten meats are documented, all of the livestock that Julie feeds upon will always be labeled with the words: 'Vampire Bitten.'

"The remaining concerns are those regarding personal safety.

"Because this topic has national ramifications, the President of the United States of America, will address these concerns and more."

The President of the United States immediately entered the White House press room. First, he thanked members of Congress for their support in dealing with the issues challenging our nation.

Next came praise for the Surgeon General and his "medically reassuring, scientifically documented statements."

He then told the nation: "My immediate concern is for the safety of Julie Wynn and her family and their neighbors... and I am equally concerned for all Santa Maria residents and visitors... and even more... for all Americans!

"My concern is based upon the fact that even before today's revelation, fanatics have openly called for this child's murder, hiding behind the Holy Bible and other religious scriptures in a perverted attempt to justify the terrorist acts they want to commit... in the hope of serving evil... even while they hypocritically claim otherwise!

"We all know that the more innocent people these evil terrorist fanatics kill and maim, the happier they will be!

"I therefore call upon all Christians and believers in all faiths, and all non-believers too, to join with me in doing everything we can to stop these terrorist fanatics from harming anyone in Santa Maria or anywhere else in our great nation, or in the world.

"I now pose to all Americans, the ultimate question.

"For centuries, we have claimed that we are the most civilized and tolerant nation in a way that no other nation on Earth has ever been.

"Therefore, I submit to you that Julie Wynn is the ultimate test of our claim.

"The life she lives will be proof of our ability to be civilized towards those who are different... or it will become the ultimate proof of our failure. The ultimate proof of the hypocrisy of our claim.

"My fellow Americans. I have faith in your ability to show the world that we are a civilized nation that tolerates differences... as long as those differences are not used as an excuse to commit acts of terrorism and other foul perversions that deprive even one person of the rights and freedoms all Americans cherish.

"The right to life, liberty, and the pursuit of happiness!

"To this end, this afternoon, I am submitting to Congress, legislation to achieve these goals. I am also submitting legislation that will provide additional safeguards to stabilize and restore our nation and our economy in the wake of the GMO panic.

"Finally, Ms. Julie Wynn. As President of the United States, I have the unique honor of formally acknowledging your existence as a vampire and to assure you and your family that I, and all of the members of this great government of the United States, will do everything in our power to protect the rights and privileges that are yours by virtue of being American citizens.

"I praise God and I pray always that His Will be done! Thank you."

At the time, I was about two months shy of my twelfth birthday, so I was old enough to understand what was happening, but not really what it meant.

However, the fact that the President of the United States had come on television and spoken about my sister, and expressed his concerns for us, and for Santa Maria, and stated his intent to work with Congress to protect us, was awesome and stunning, for none of us knew that he was going to speak at this press conference.

Still, we remained composed and listened to the news summations and commentaries before watching "the family of Julie interview" that had been taped last night.

Here I must make a confession: Seeing myself and my family on television was different from what I was expecting.

On one hand, it was like watching the home videos mom and dad had made down through the years.

On the other hand, there were news statements and commentaries before and after, along with the realization that everyone in the world was likely watching these newscasts and our interview.

Of course what we saw was a replay of last night's events with no editing or interruptions.

Just us in the living room shortly after Julie awakened, prior to leaving for the ranch so she could have her nightly cow.

After being introduced to our local television news reporter, Ms. Renner, Julie sat on mom's lap.

The first question was: "Julie. Are you a vampire?"

Julie corrected: "Girl and vampire."

Mom explained that since Julie had just turned two, she was still learning words and attempting to link concepts: "We have told her that she is a girl and a vampire, but her understanding is that of any two year old. She really does not understand what a vampire is…"

Julie interrupted: "Vampire no food."

Her words and mom's mechanical reinforcement: "Vampires are not food," proved mom's assertion and for the sake of video verification, mom coaxed Julie to open her mouth wide.

Julie did, revealing ivory white incisors that were long, thin, and decidedly razor-sharp.

Those teeth were irrefutable and undeniable proof that God had indeed given life to one of mankind's greatest imaginary fears.

Imaginary because until now, there had been no confirmation of human vampires, prompting Ms. Renner to ask: "Is the thought of Julie's being a vampire and feeding on blood acceptable to you?"

Dad shrugged: "Feeding is normal and we all live off of something. We kill plants and we kill animals, then we eat them. Julie never kills animals because then, she cannot feed off of them again... but she does feed off of them. Is either kind of feeding wrong?"

After a pause so all could reflect upon the morality issue dad had just presented, mom added: "During the time Julie was struggling to feed on formula and ever since... even when she was very hungry... she never once attempted to bite anyone or drink our blood."

Mom then asked Julie: "Are you hungry?"

"Want cow now!"

"Are people food?"

Julie's decree had finality saturating every word: "People no food."

For the sake of the public record and to protect me from being harassed in school, Dad asked: "Is your brother Leo food?"

"Eeoo no food."

"Tiny, the dog. Is he food?"

"Snack!"

"What is food?"

"Cow!"

The questioning headed elsewhere and I was gratefully that "Eeoo stink" had not been mentioned, for I had horrors of having that phrase haunt me for the remainder of my school days.

Still, I briefly became the center of attention: "Leo. Is it true that your sister smelled in your scent, the fact that you were unknowingly dangerously ill, and that this saved your life?"

"Yes," I shyly admitted, then lapsed into silence, so mom jumped in: "When the veterinarians confirmed that the cows Julie pointed out, were sick, Julie's statement that Leo also smelled sick, was cause for concern, so the doctors examined him and discovered a life threatening blood clot in his brain."

Dad took over: "The doctors discovered it while it was so small that they were able to treat it with medications rather than surgery. Follow-up exams have confirmed that the medications are working and that he will not need surgery. The cure is expected to final with no complications and no likelihood of reoccurrence because it was spotted so early thanks to Julie."

Ms. Renner turned to Julie: "What is your favorite toy?"

"Brownie," Julie decreed since she had recently shifted her Chomp Neck attentions from the giraffe to the horse.

Mom swiftly jumped in: "She has just awakened so she is very hungry. After she feeds, she enjoys playing with the kinds of toys all two year olds do, and she is a very sociable little girl."

At the mention of the word "hungry" Julie interrupted: "Want cow now!" so on a whim, I lifted Julie from mom's lap.

Holding her so her head was at shoulder lever, I exposed my neck and asked: "Want food?"

"You no food!" came the irate protest: "Want cow!"

It was the perfect protest and the ideal way to end this interview.

Since Julie had just turned two, she was totally unaware of the interview and the uproar that her existence was unleashing.

She was even more unaware that she was now an excuse for the fears some people avidly wanted to feel.

For her at the time, all that mattered could be summed up in two words and she made certain that Tiny learned them soon after her May eleventh feeding.

Suddenly, Tiny found himself being floored by the humming two year old, who this time, was content to suck upon the vanquished neck rather than bite it, even as she told him: "Nice cowie."

THE STREET LEGAL WAR

During the days following the revelation that Julie was a vampire, the news media had a field day.

Here is a sampling of the headlines:

"Cow Feeding Vampire Born To Humans!"

"Vampire Saves Orcutt Herds And More!"

"FDA & Surgeon General Fund Vampire Research."

"Vampires: The Medical Miracle Machine?"

"Congress Grapples With Constitutional Vampire Questions."

"Scientists Search For Other Vampires. Are Dogs Key To Finding Them?"

"Will Vampire Bites Lead To Arthritis Cures?"

"Vampire Laws Hotly Debated!"

"Money In The Blood Or Blood Money? An Expose."

"Vampire Stuns The World!"

"The Economics Of Vampires. A Critical Review Of Potential Impacts."

"GMOs & Vampires. Wall Street's Reaction."

"Vampire Debate Reaches NATO & The United Nations."

"Transylvania! Romania's Vampire Heritage: Fact Or Fiction?"

"Religions Debate Vampire Issue. Schisms Likely!"

"What Vampires Eat! The Shocking Truth!" is still mom and dad's favorite because the answer was cow's blood.

"Toddling Two Year Old Vampire Strikes Fear In The Hearts Of Fanatics!" will always be my all time favorite.

Even now, I can envision my two year old sister toddling down the street chasing a herd of fleeing fanatics.

This was when the news media began paying regular visits to our home and the second reporter in the door was Max Smillet, since the television team he had earlier edged out, had interviewed us for the public revelation.

This was when tasteful videos of Julie's feedings were broadcast and Tom's "Spooky Cool" was revealed in context.

Meanwhile, in my elementary school, television confirmation that my sister sleeps in our garage in a stone structure nicknamed "the castle" was the ultimate vindication.

It verified that childhood fantasies could be real and my sister the vampire, was living proof!

This sentiment was confirmed when martial law was lifted and school resumed on May sixteenth.

"Leo! Is your sister really a vampire?"

"Yea."

"With fangs and everything?"

"Yea."

"Spooky Cool! Was that really you on television?"

"Yea."

"Awesome! ...and she sleeps in the garage?"

"Yea."

"Wow! I wish mine did!"

"Yea."

The first round of this series of questions was okay.

The next three billion repeats were not.

Yes, I am exaggerating a little when I say billion, but that is what it felt like. The same questions, in almost the same order, each and every time! This made "yea" the perfect answer because then, I only had to half listen to the questions, while struggling to not fall asleep or turn brain dead.

It should be noted that the female wish to exile their brothers to the garage was equally strong, but they at least wanted to learn things.

"Is she cute?" "Does she play with dolls?" "What's her favorite toy? Game? Clothing? Color?" "Is she shy?" "Does she like to cuddle?" "Are her fangs scary or cute?" "Can she come to school so we can meet her?"

To the last question, I answered: "Sunlight hurts her too much for her to come out during the day, or even early sunset."

Their disappointment was obvious because they really wanted to meet her, and thankfully, this wish was soon granted.

Unfortunately, there were a few boys and girls who were sometimes vile.

Their questions included: "Do you go to church?"

"Did you pray to Jesus to protect you from the devil?"

"Did your parents read the bible before she was born?"

"Has she been baptized?"

"Does she grin when she sucks blood?"

"Do you suck blood?"

Except for the last two questions, questions like these were okay.

The problem was that these kids did not care what the answers were, unless it was an answer they wanted, or an answer they could twist for their own selfish ends.

Going to church did not count at all, unless it was the church they went to, and they proclaimed that having Julie baptized was evil because they believed that she was Satan's creation and that baptizing her was immoral.

Yet had I said that she had not been baptized, then I and my family would have been accused of being unchristian, and even I could see that the only reason they asked if she grinned during feeding, was because they wanted her to be their idea of evil, so I answered: "She eats just like you do."

"I am not a bloodsucker!"

"You're worse than a bloodsucker. Jesus said not to judge and if you really love Jesus, you would obey Him and His commandments and not judge me or my sister or my family... but you are! That makes you a hypocrite and hypocrites only serve Satan."

This phrase was one of several that my parents helped me to memorize, knowing in advance that I would need them to protect myself and my family from precisely these kind of hypocrites.

Naturally those kids refused to even consider the Biblical truth in those words.

Instead, they mechanically proclaimed: "I do not believe in Satan!"

I countered: "If you really believed in God, you would accept the fact that He is the creator of all, just like the Holy Bible says. Instead, you make Satan, God's equal by claiming that he has the power to create. The Holy Bible says that the only power Satan has is to lie and deceive, but you would rather believe the satanic lie that Satan is God's equal... than admit that God created my sister!"

My parents had also given me these words and after I used them and others, like the hypocrite statement, the vile kids began keeping their distance.

This was when they began creating and spreading lies and rumors to the point where I had no choice but to realize a very simple truth.

Their words, deeds, and hatred, were proof that they worshipped Satan in their actual actions and beliefs.

As for the creation of those rumors, they were so thoroughly documented that the school board had to issue an injunction proclaiming that this kind of lying would be punished, as would racist and sexist remarks.

The vile kids and their families too, then proclaimed that they were being persecuted because they were Christian, but this injunction finally shut them up and the rumors instantly stopped.

This was the ultimate proof of their source.

These experiences forced me to become religious in the sense that I finally realized how supremely correct Jesus was when in reference to His teachings in the Sermon on the Mount, He asked: "Why call you me Lord, Lord, and not do the things I say?"

Then He repeatedly commanded: "If you would be my disciple, follow my commandments!"

The commandments on behavior He issued, includes not lying and not judging, which includes not making up false stories and decreeing that someone is evil because of those fantasies.

Sadly, that was what began happening from the first day back at school, and I wish I did not have to write about this kind of stuff, but I do because it did happen.

Further proof was that these same vile kids said that God was punishing my family by "making them be the parents of a vampire" because my best friend Tom, is black.

They probably said this because they did not yet know about my distant gay relative, but need I even mention the vile racist things they said about Tom?

They said equally untrue and profane things about my Hispanic friends, Carlos and Juan, and about my Asian friends, Steven and Mitch too.

Those remarks almost got them permanently expelled from school and thankfully, the vile kids were in the minority.

The majority of the kids, including those from non fanatic Christian families, swiftly rejected the vile kids once they realized what was happening, and this support made it easier to cope with school and the Street Legal War.

The Street Legal War began on Wednesday, May 18, 2011, when a group of fanatics gathered on the sidewalk fronting the car dealership where my dad worked.

Since he was reasonably well known, his place of work was no secret, hence the fanatics had made posters, then began picketing the dealership.

Thanks to newspapers, magazines, and the internet, photos of my dad were easy to come by, enabling them to plaster his picture on picket signs, along with their judgmental proclamations.

These included: "Servant of Satan!" "Don't buy a car from this Bloodsucker!" "This Monster only wants your blood!" "This Man Worships The Antichrist!" and of course: "Vampire Lover!"

Mom later said that they picked on the wrong man because dad's stars confirm that he is a full blooded Taurus who has no hesitation about fighting back.

Therefore, instead of running and hiding, dad told his boss: "Times are tight. We need all of the advertising we can get... so let's use it!"

His plan was the one they ran with.

Starting with Santa Maria, they called every newspaper, radio, and television station, in Santa Barbara and San Luis Obispo counties.

When the timing was right, they called the police.

The police immediately began their investigation and because my dad was being targeted, the FBI also investigated.

Since the protest was peaceful, the fanatics were not immediately arrested, but they were warned: "You run the risk of being arrested or sued for slander and libel, and for violating equal rights laws and possibly other laws as well."

This did not stop the fanatics, since being martyred for their cause was acceptable and in their own eyes, they could do no wrong.

However, the counterattack had only just begun.

Within the hour, freshly painted banners were posted around the dealership: "Fanatic Specials!" "Protester Discounts!" "Monster Deals!" and "In God We Trust!"

These banners were photographed by the news media, as were the judgmental protest signs, even while the dealership was swiftly updating its television, radio, newspaper, and internet, advertising. Under the heading of "Protester Specials!" car photos included captions like: "This Car Won't Suck Your Blood Or Your Wallet!" "The AB Positive Car!" "Midnight Special!" "Love at First Bite!" along with the tag line: "We bleed for you!"

The dealership was even faster to team up with blood banks to host blood drives and they advertised this too.

However, what pushed this story into the limelight was the on-site television interview conducted by Santa Maria's local station because the unscripted live interview was a classic.

The leader of the picketing fanatics was interviewed by Ms. Renner, who inquired: "Why are you picketing this automobile dealership?"

"We are protesting because a salesman who works here has a daughter who is the genuine handiwork of Satan! An evil perversion who has the power to destroy the whole world!"

"Can you tell us what makes his daughter so evil?"

"She is a vampire! A satanic bloodsucker!"

At the time, Ms. Renner was involved in a heated tax dispute with the Internal Revenue Service, the IRS, so she unthinkingly asked: "If you are going after bloodsuckers, shouldn't you also be picketing the IRS?"

With a perfectly straight face, the fanatic responded: "We could never do that, because they are street legal bloodsuckers!"

The words: "Street Legal Bloodsuckers" became an instant sensation. Bumper stickers, posters, and monogrammed T-shirt sales were off the charts.

The IRS took this phrase to heart and it became their informal motto. In jest, they later sent letters to Ms. Renner and the fanatic, thanking them for the motto.

Meanwhile, belatedly realizing what had just been said, Ms. Renner reacted with a knee-jerk question: "If the government legalizes the car salesman's daughter, will the protest stop?"

The fanatic froze as if he had been slapped in the face, then angrily retorted: "You cannot legalize Satan's spawn! Especially a cowsucker!"

Though the interview ended then and there, Ms. Renner became an overnight celebrity for having asked the right questions, thus advancing her career and transforming this event from a local news story, into a nationwide sensation that fascinated the entire world.

Even countries who were attempting to use the vampire story to end or redefine their relationships with the United States, aired it repeatedly.

It was also a commentator's dream come true and the editorial spin-offs seemed endless.

As for what could be legalized, most people felt that governments were living proof of precisely what could be legalized.

GMOs and corporate greed were deemed the ultimate proofs.

As you know from direct experience, the term "cowsucker" became an overnight sensation replacing many previously overused four letter words, and the dealership swiftly added: "Hot Cow Specials!" "Street Legal Specials!" "We Know Bloodsuckers And How To Avoid Them!" and "Don't Let This Cow Scare You!" to the growing list of counter advertising.

Each time the dealership made a sale, a small black and white paper cow was posted on the wall and on its internet page. When dad made the sale, the cow was brown and at the end of the day, the cow tallies were announced.

Soon thereafter, small cow flags were flying from the dealer's lamp poles and a complementary cow flag was given to each purchaser.

Then the Street Legal War escalated.

It began when the massive increase in dealership car sales on the eighteenth and nineteenth, fostered by news media coverage of the protest, prompted the fanatics to up their rhetoric and protest the manufacturer of the new cars that the dealership sold.

Late on the nineteenth, they called upon "All True Believers" to boycott this manufacturer and its dealerships.

They promoted this boycott nationwide.

The manufacturer countered with nationwide advertising akin to what the dealership was doing and ultimately, the boycotts were deemed unsuccessful, since the counter reaction was a threefold increase in sales. Many purchases were publicly acknowledged to have been made in protest against the fanatics.

In those difficult economic times, that was indeed newsworthy.

Equally newsworthy was the anti fanatic protest that had mobilized.

Now standing near the original protesters were those carrying signs in support of my dad and the dealership.

These read: "Stop Giving Religion A Bad Name!" "Fanatics Serve Satan!" "Boycott Hate Mongers! Go To A Real Church!" "They have nothing to offer but fear, lies, and profanity!" and the most famous of all: "Better A Cowsucker Than A Hypocrite!"

Many protesters wore T-shirts with cows on them and a few of those cows had improvised fangs drawn on them.

As dad noted: "Civility would have been in short supply had the police and the news media not been present."

Then came the stunning news.

On May twenty third, the police announced that the organizers of the original protest had family members who owned a competing car dealership in Santa Maria and some of the picketers had family members who worked at that dealership.

The police therefore decreed that this protest was nothing more than an illegal attempt to steal business from a competing dealership using religion as a cover for unlawful activities.

This led to multiple arrests and charges of unfair and deceptive business practices, discrimination with intent to harm, plus slander and libel.

These charges and more were leveled locally and nationwide as numerous state and federal district attorneys instigated prosecutions and lawsuits, some on behalf of my dad since the fanatic attacks had been aimed at him personally.

Other lawsuits were issued on behalf of the manufacturer whose cars had been targeted by the boycott, and the dealership again took the offensive: "They cannot compete against our excellent cars so they picketed us!" "They have so little to offer that they have to lie and deceive in order to win your business!" and "Who even needs to lie except Satan's minions?"

The arrests and the legitimately adverse news did much to quiet the initial fanatic outburst, including at school where the retort created by my classmates: "Cowsucking Lawbreakers!" further isolated the fanatic kids.

Thus by May twenty fifth, a relative level of normality had been restored. At least at the dealership, though the cow flags and sales slogans were maintained.

On the home front, some of the local kids, mostly my friends and their sisters, began teaching Julie a game that my parents hoped would lessen her preoccupation with Chomp Neck.

The game was Hide and Seek and in the beginning, Julie was not very good at hiding because she hummed whenever an alluring neck came into view.

As for seeking, it was impossible to hide from her and we were baffled until mom reminded us: "She has a very keen sense of smell."

After that, we mostly limited her to hiding, which had an unintended consequence for once Julie learned to stop humming, she became very skilled at hiding and she used this skill to become an even more formidable Chomp Neck player.

Thus while playing Hide and Seek, we never knew when we were going to become Chomp Neck victims and those hiding were as much at risk as was the seeker.

In response, mom patiently reminded us: "Julie is still only two and she has to learn to become a skilled vampire too."

Resigned, we put up Julie's version of Hide and Hum-Chomp, and my friends' sisters gave Julie the girl time she enjoyed and wanted as much as mom enjoyed having neighborhood parents over for visits.

This made for a growing sense of calm, though there were still a few bumps and potholes in the road.

This time complements of mom, albeit indirectly.

During a magazine interview, the fact that as a baby, Julie went for necks when she was hungry, was brought up since the government felt it was the time to document that this was no longer an issue.

Mom obliged by declaring: "Once Julie finally got the food she needed and was no longer starving to death, she stopped necking."

True to form, she said this with a perfectly straight face and a week passed before she belatedly realized what she had unintentionally implied.

By then it was too late for the phrase had been printed and its many variants were avidly and gleefully in use nationwide.

Still, the issue of the moment was that aside from those who knew our family, and the kids who had been visiting us since before the revelation, there were a few parents who did not want their children to come over to my house to play with me, due to fear of my sister.

Some adults were fearful too.

One man even refused to walk his dog past our house during the day, out of fear that the vampire might want a drink from his dog despite the reported health benefits and the fact that Julie could only come out at night.

In sharp contrast, the kids were fascinated by Julie.

The possibility that she might bite one of the other children and they could watch, appealed to them.

They were deeply disappointed when they learned that Julie did not and would not drink human blood.

Still, this confirmation did little to decrease the imaginary fears and mom tried to fight them by noting during a newspaper interview: "Like all children, she needs friends to play with. The more the better. This is how children learn to socialize and if this does not happen, she will not come to think of them as friends and playmates."

This time, mom said nothing improper, but the fanatics jumped on the word "playmate" decreeing that the use of this "sex term" was not accidental, any more than was the word "necking."

This added imaginary immorality to the long list of false accusations.

Even after the news media aired ample documentation showing the fanatics and especially their religious leaders, using the word "playmate" to refer to childhood interactions, the distant howling of those rabid wolves continued.

Thankfully they would not seriously plague us for a while and other matters kept us more than preoccupied.

COWS NEED LIGHT!

The other events that rounded out the fateful month of May, 2011, were the government's doing.

They needed scientific results, fast, in order to verify the claims that had been made. Thus they began providing cows and later a dog that they needed Julie to bite.

The cows were initially brought to the ranch, including an arthritic cow that Julie was asked to feed upon several times, and she did.

There was also a cow that they wanted her to bite because its bloodline came from a long line of cattle bred solely for research.

To everyone's surprise, she refused: "No want hurt!"

In response, the animal was examined and found to have a weak heart, further verifying that Julie is vampire who does not want to hurt living beings.

However the fact that this cow did not stink, roused questions, so the cow was offered the next evening, evoking the same protest: "No want hurt!"

"Julie. Does this cow stink?"

"Cow no stink."

"Then how can feeding hurt it?"

"Cow hurt."

"Is the cow in pain?"

"Cow in pain."

The medical assumption was that Julie could smell pain so the cow was given medication to relieve the pain.

Once it took hold she was asked: "Is the cow in pain?"

"No."

"Will feeding hurt it?"

"Yes."

"Why?"

Julie struggled to find the needed words: "Cow talk bad."

Since the cow had been silent the entire, time everyone was baffled by her words, but because I had recently been on the receiving end of Hide and Hum-Chomp, I had a sudden suspicion and tested it.

Putting her head next to my chest, I asked: "Do you hear my heart going thump, thump?"

"Hear heart."

"Does the cow's heart talk bad?"

"Heart talk bad!"

I was the hero of the moment, for I had discovered how superior my sister's hearing was, which led to the idea of testing her vision.

Doing so was a minor mistake.

At the ranch, pictures of different shapes: Triangles, Circles, and Squares, were mounted on posts set at varying distances.

Each lighted.

Seated next to each post was a man who had a walkie-talkie who listened for the code that told him when to stand up or sit down.

Julie was told: "When a man stands up, touch the picture on this table that looks like the picture next to the man."

The table's placement assured that Julie was standing in a fixed spot. Hence the distance from where she was, to each post, was known, so her visual abilities could be calculated.

As expected, Julie had no trouble seeing each man stand and she pointed to the corresponding picture on the table.

Then came the mistake: The lights were turned off.

This change did not bother Julie in the least.

In fact, she liked it because she could see far better when the lights were off and now that she knew they could be turned off, that was what she wanted all of the time.

"Light off please," became her favorite phrase and while those at the ranch could nullify her request by saying: "Cows need light!" at home, this excuse did not work.

Nor did: "We need light!" or "Tiny needs light!"

Thanks to her keen intelligence, Julie swiftly learned how to turn lights off, and thanks to her strength, she could use a hand on the wall to steady herself, then jump high enough to turn them off.

Since most switches in our house were positioned where she could reach them, Hide and Seek took a new turn, because Julie would turn off the lights in the room where she hid.

She also turned them off when she entered a room to search it.

Naturally, remembering to turn them on again was something no two year old would even think to do, and this applied even more to Julie, since she did not need them at all.

Not even to look at pictures, so mom, dad, and I, and all visitors too, began carrying flashlights around the house in order to cope with ongoing, unannounced Julie outages.

Even now, I can hear dad thundering in the sudden darkness: "Julie! Turn the light back on... now!"

Mom just turned on her flashlight, walked over the switch, turned it on, then told the girl: "Leave it on, please."

The other problematic issue was that once Julie discovered cows, she had no desire to feed upon anything else.

Despite snack threats, Julie was content to play Chomp Neck with Tiny, but she felt no desire to feed on him or any other dog.

At least not for the moment.

This did not help the cause of science because the doctors and researchers needed her to bite the arthritic dog they had acquired so they could study the results.

In the end, the dog was brought to our house and mom announced: "The cows are not home tonight, so this dog was brought for you to feed on."

Eventually, hunger won out over hardnosed insistence upon the cow and Julie fed, but this time there was a difference.

Shortly before sunrise, she needed a second feeding and since this need caught everyone by surprise, Tiny was volunteered.

This meant that more than one dog at a time would be needed, which the doctors preferred since it would give them more animals to study, and Julie's bites did indeed eliminate arthritis pain in both the dog and the cow.

Still, the reality was that Julie now needed to feed on larger animals and cows were best since only one feeding a day was needed.

This limited research to cows until Julie became old enough to understand what was happening and could cooperate with the doctors.

What was not problematic from the Julie standpoint, was the other major test that was implemented.

Since the doctors and the government now had the needed manpower in place, they wanted to formally confirm that Julie could smell illnesses in humans.

They did this by arranging for her to visit my elementary school in the evening over seven days to meet with each grade level.

The official reason was so she could begin learning about school and meet other kids and let them meet her.

The real reason was so she could point out the stinky ones.

Therefore, on Wednesday, May twenty fifth, a cow was delivered to our house and placed in our backyard to expedite feeding.

Then we walked Julie to the school.

The first night, it was Kindergarten and Julie was curious and shy because classrooms were new to her and she had never seen this many kids before.

Each grade level averaged just over ninety kids, which meant well over three hundred people, from family, teachers, medical, and government personnel, to news media reporters since this event was naturally being recorded.

This time, live on television and Julie did not disappoint.

Her unique hums revealed her curiosity, while the fact that she stayed close to mom and dad after being set on her feet, confirmed her shyness.

Long moments later, one of the older Kindergarteners walked up and said: "Hello Julie. I am Heather. Are you a real vampire?"

"Girl and Vampire." Julie insisted, then she turned and buried her head in mom's skirt.

Mom knelt and attempted to coax away the shyness: "Julie... Heather wants to be a friend. Do you want to be a friend?"

"Yes."

"Then what do you say?"

"Light off please."

"The lights need to stay on when people are in school... but you can say hello."

Julie's "hello" was so neutral that mom took over: "Hello, Heather. I am happy to meet you. I am Mrs. Wynn and this is my daughter, Julie. Julie, there are animals on the counter. Would you like Heather to show them to you?"

As Heather led the way, Julie stayed close to mom.

She was fascinated by the mice and hamsters and eagerly held them, but the snake did not interest her at all because to her, snakes: "No smell nice."

This was probably not what the fanatics wanted to hear.

As soon as Julie was comfortable, dad held her and asked: "Does anyone smell sick?"

Mom and dad had been encouraging her to say "sick" instead of "stink," and she answered: "Yes."

"Can you point them out to me?"

"Yes," so dad walked where Julie pointed and she guided him to three children who smelled: "Little sick."

She also pointed to one teacher, three family members, and a medical aide, telling each: "Yes sick."

Each was immediately scheduled for a free medical checkup at the hospital, since this assessment was being done to find anything and everything that might be wrong.

On the news the next evening, the announcement that all whom Julie identified, had indeed been afflicted, was enhanced by doctor statements that early treatment would spare them the brunt of their illnesses.

The fact that one adult had barely detectable cancer that was caught almost before it began, meant that more students and family were there when she visited first grade, later that evening.

By the time the last visit ended with Julie's tour of my sixth grade classroom, she was comfortable with the crowd and her performance more than exceeded medical expectations.

Eighty three people had been detected, including a news camera man, plus two kids and a parent who were of the fanatic persuasion.

Tragically, the afflicted fanatic and the fanatic parents of the two afflicted children, refused to allow the doctors to examine them: "We will not be a part of this satanic scam!"

The government in turn, mandated that the parents sign liability releases so they could not sue the doctors, because Julie had said: "Yes sick" to the girl and "More sick" when pointing to the boy.

Within two months the boy was diagnosed with brain cancer that would have likely been treatable, had they allowed him to be examined at the time. But it was less than a week before the girl was hospitalized due to the severity of the flu.

Her fanatic parents then publicly proclaimed that Julie had cursed their daughter and the government responded by charging them with slander, and forcing them to prove their claim in court.

The fact that the parents had not allowed their daughter to be tested after Julie made her decree, plus the fact that the fanatic adult who refused to let himself be tested, had died of a sudden but treatable stroke, undercut their "she cursed them" claim before the trial even began.

On the other hand, for the doctors, and most people too, the fact that Julie was accurately spotting illnesses, some life threatening, went a long way to proving that she was not the monster that many of them had initially imagined.

As for the girl in my class named Julie, who had recently stopped giving me such a hard time in school. On June third, she told me: "Your sister is way more than cute! She's adorable!"

I nodded in agreement, not quite ready to forget all of the mean things that this Julie had said over the past three and a half years.

However, what I thought at the time, was that my sister was cute because she did not have to live with her.

The medical appointment in which the doctors said I was cured, had occurred on Saturday morning, May twenty eighth.

That same evening, we went to the Gentry's home, whereupon Julie decided that it was time for a game of Chomp Neck.

Naturally without warning.

After she bagged Tom, catching all of us completely by surprise, Tom looked at me and said: "At least you're safe cause Eeoo stink."

With an expression only a brother or sister would even think to have, Julie gleefully declared: "Eeoo no stink! Eeoo smell!"

The fact that Julie's foul smelling outputs had vanished within weeks after she began eating properly, meant that countering by saying that she also stank, would have made me look stupid.

Thus, I responded the only way I could: "Thanks a lot, fang face!"

"Leo!"

"Mom!"

Dad reminded me: "Thank God for the fact that you don't stink!"

Susan chuckled: "Face it, Leo. You are a marked man."

Actually we all were, but none of us knew it just yet.

A 1-800-VAMPIRE

At home, things were relatively quiet for just over a year.

Tom and I were now in junior high school and wondering how it was even possible to have once considered elementary school to be so difficult, while Julie was exploring her world as only an older two year old can.

We were now zoned to keep a cow or two in our backyard, which meant feedings at home. This made everyone in the family happier, though having a cow delivered straight to our door, then picked up after being fed upon, gave home delivery a whole new meaning.

By this time, Julie and my parents were being paid to take her to local cattle ranches so she could inspect the herds.

There were of course, weekly visits to the hospital screening clinic, so she could spot those who were ill.

Around this time, we learned that Julie's bites were not the least bit harmful for those feeding on the meat of the animals she fed upon.

In fact it was just the opposite.

Arthritis sufferers had decreases in their symptoms and others with medical conditions including asthma, seemed to benefit.

Yet even more notable was and still is the flavor.

When Julie feeds on an animal, its meat is enhanced in a manner that is truly memorable, giving rise to the growing likelihood that the "Certified Vampire Bitten" label Paul had predicted, would soon become a reality.

That is, once the government felt that enough time and testing had passed to calm public fears.

Meanwhile, the researchers were going crazy.

Meat samples from the cows Julie bit were as unrevealing as her salvia samples. Yet if she just hummed repeatedly at a cow, nothing changed, so they knew it was the bites.

Testing that she was able to cooperate with shortly before she turned three, documented that she was not injecting anything into the meat. Only feeding, but just bleeding animals of the small amounts of blood she consumed, roughly eight ounces, did not change the flavor of the animals who were bled.

Then, as if to verify the complexity of the puzzle, six months after last being fed upon, Tiny had a recurrence of his arthritis, so we coaxed Julie into forgoing her nightly cow and feeding on him.

She did and the cameras confirmed how fast the relief came despite the fact that neither before or after blood samples revealed anything meaningful just yet.

Something was there.

It was just playing very hard to get.

Equally interesting were the space age materials that were tested to see if they would give Julie a measure of protection from sunlight.

Many did and best of all, were the materials used to shield space shuttles, space stations, and satellites.

Nothing came close to giving her the protection that hard stone provided, but a stone shelter covered by space age materials was light enough to be placed on a trailer, enabling her to be transported in safety, knowing that if something went wrong, sheltering her would not be problematic.

This enabled us to make nighttime visits to the Santa Barbara Zoo, and the Charles Paddock Zoo in Atascadero, leading to the discovery that there are animals that Julie refuses to feed upon.

Caribous and gnus yes, zebras no.

Cheetahs and lions no, tigers yes.

Of course, this list is far longer and Julie spotted a raccoon and a parrot that were on the verge of becoming ill, but ultimately, thanks to these Zoo outings, the researchers now realized that she was not the vampire equivalent of an omnivore.

She would not feed on just anything and this might include domestic animals.

Therefore, they set up a domestic zoo and after her nightly cow, we were driven to the farm where these animals were gathered.

The findings are still true today.

To Julie, dairy cattle are okay, but she does not consider them to be food because they smell too much like Zebras and horses, which is amusing, since dairy cattle are derived from beef cattle.

She ranks sheep with most dog breeds and goats, though goats are way down on her list and since at the time, she had cows, she expressed no interest in those animals.

Llamas fascinate her more than any other animal and she adores their smell like we enjoy flowers, but she refuses to feed on them.

If she was starving, chickens, turkeys, and geese, might interest her, which puts them in the same category as several domestic cat breeds, but there is one animal she wants nothing to do with, ever.

Pigs, because to Julie: "Pigs smell like people."

This led to a "Smell the Human" experiment.

Much to the disappointment of fanatics and racists, all humans smell the same as far as Julie is concerned.

Beyond individual differences, the human scent is universally the same and it does not matter what a person eats.

To her, vegetarians smell the same as excessive pork or garlic eaters. As for garlic and onions, those scents mean nothing to her. She ranks them with flowers, grass, and water.

On the amusing side, even after the publication of the "garlic fact," garlic growers still made tons of money off of those who were fearful or superstitious. Among the fanatics, garlic jewelry, garlic scented guard dogs, and garlic coated bullets, were big sellers.

Anyway, the reality is that Julie can feed on some, but not all animals and her food of choice is beef cattle, and later, sheep.

However, even then, she is actually very picky.

She can smell genetically modified animals and animals that have been fed GMOs and she refuses to feed on them.

When grass fed cows and sheep are available, she will not feed on animals that have been fed corn or other feeds.

Thus Paul's joke about "Vampire Approved" is absolutely correct, because if Julie likes it, it is organic and grass fed.

Obviously, Julie loves going to zoos because of the many diverse scents, and equally pleasurable are outings to rivers and streams.

She enjoys watching and listening to running water and she would have run up the water bill, had dad not bought her mini fountain.

Thanks to the researchers, we soon learned that fountains that gurgle like streams or sound like rain, are her favorites and watching and listening to one can still keep her happily preoccupied.

However, what she loves most of all is the beach.

When she first saw the ocean and its waves, she squealed and hummed in delight and though she does not want to leave the beach, when mom or dad says: "Dawn will come soon. It's time to go home," she sadly, swiftly complies, documenting her ongoing awareness of what sunlight does to her.

Given these events and more, dad mused during her birthday party on March 29, 2012: "She has survived and is doing just fine."

I quipped: "What about us?"

I was the one closest to the mark because 2012 would become progressively more challenging, but not due to Julie.

The only Julie personal issue was the establishment of an evening preschool so she could attend class and play with children her own age, outside of the home, which did not occur until the Fall of 2012.

When it finally came, what was eye-opening were the differences.

Language wise, she was now only a little ahead, but when it came to physical abilities, this three year old was in a different world.

She was faster, stronger, quicker, and more coordinated, but even more, she was extremely aware of all that went on around her.

Thus, none of the kids were able to do things like sneak up on her, or surprise her with a sudden blow, or hair pulling.

Most likely thanks to her keen hearing and sense of smell.

Still, what the researchers noted most of all, was her gentleness and shyness. The fact that she retreats from confrontations, rather than standing her ground, and the only exceptions at the time, were Chomp Neck and her Hum-Chomp version of Hide and Seek.

Games she only played at home.

Perhaps this explained my ongoing intense desire to have sleepovers at Tom's house.

These realities allowed us to focus on the political firestorm of 2012, for it was a Presidential election year and none of the candidates at any level, had any real issues that they could use to differentiate themselves.

The reason was that political and economic circumstances no longer permitted it.

The public had long ago made up its mind about GMOs, so any politician who did not take a hardline stand against them would be struggling to get their own family to cast even a single vote for them.

Equally known was that any politician who did not genuinely deliver on their anti GMO promises would be lucky if they were only lynched by the angry mob.

Just as cast in stone was the economy. People were no longer swayed by corporate news media propaganda on behalf of the wealthy. The mood was now: Tax the rich and the corporations. End corporate welfare and government giveaways. Give us the social services, the secure retirement, and the single-payer not-for-profit medical coverage that all of the other industrialized countries in the world have long had, and do it immediately!

Since failure to do these things in the United States would have likely resulted in a three hundred million people revolt, the handwriting was finally on the wall and even the corporations knew better than to fight it. At least not openly, so beyond trade and rebuilding the economy, this left only one hot button topic.

The vampire and what to do about her.

In retrospect, the President was running for reelection and he had the commanding advantage since his record was proven.

All he needed to say was: "More of the same! The research is continuing. The tremendous health benefits she has already provided to the community and ranchers are amply documented!"

Of course the language was fancier and far longer, as political speechwriters struggled to find four hundred and twenty seven ways to say the same old thing between January first and election day, while making it sound new and different each time.

This left incumbent candidates with an easy choice. Support the President on the vampire issue, or take a different stand.

Most chose support because in the eyes of the vast majority, Julie was a cute adorable little vampire.

This left the opposing candidates with only three options. Be more pro vampire, or agree with the President, or become anti vampire to a greater or lesser degree.

The man challenging the incumbent President, took an anti vampire stance, making Julie the first three year old in history to become the topic of debate in a major political campaign.

The anti vampire platform was based on the premise that Julie was not a threat, but that safeguards and security measures needed to be far beyond what had been done to date.

During one debate, the challenger thundered: "Without safeguards! If something goes wrong! None of us will be safe! The GMO panic is the ultimate proof! We need more vampire security measures!"

After a lengthy list, including forcing the world's one and only vampire to have a locator chip surgically implanted, the President countered: "GMOs became problematic because no regulations and safeguards were put in place when they were first created, nor for decades afterwards.

"In total contrast... the moment Julie Wynn was brought to my attention by the medical community, I began working with scientists and medical doctors... and with professionals in the Food and Drug Administration, the Department of Agriculture, and more.

"Our goal was to create and perfect legislation that from the start, fully protects all of us... yet allows for the needed research that has been struggling to understand scientific data that no scientist in the world has ever before encountered.

"I then worked with both Political Parties in both Houses of Congress to further refine and perfect this legislation, including provisions which ensure that future concerns and needs will be rapidly assessed and swiftly dealt with.

"Do I really need to state that Julie's anatomy has features never seen in the entire history of medicine and if surgery is ever needed, it will be totally experimental because everything from her stomach to her respiratory system has differences born from her fully human genetics in a manner that is truly and utterly unique.

"That is why I asked the Surgeon General to investigate what would happen if a chip was implanted in Julie Wynn.

"After several weeks of medical assessment, he was finally able to confidently tell me: 'Mr. President, we do not know for certain, but surgery might kill her. Her blood shows responses to medications that are different from those found in children and adults who receive these same medications. Therefore surgical intervention of any kind, no matter how minor, has a very high potential of being fatal.'"

The President paused, then noted: "I would like to express my personal view... based upon prior conversations over the past year... that the esteemed Senator has no desire to harm Julie Wynn in any manner... but this does not change the fact that we need to use common sense and proven medical science, before we undertake actions that violate any person's right to life, liberty, and the pursuit of happiness!

"Yet at the same time... all people must be protected to the fullest extent possible! That is what my Administration has done when dealing with GMOs and with the economic crisis. That is precisely what I will continue doing on behalf of the American people!

"The vampire legislation I have already signed into law is proof of this pledge and it is so successful that it protects all of us and Julie Wynn too!"

This was the shortest "Julie debate" lasting a mere ten minutes, including the combative post statement exchanges. She was a topic in all four Presidential debates and in numerous skirmishes for lower offices as well.

Therefore, the one on the receiving end was my family.

The instrument of torture was the telephone.

The first year of Julie's vampire existence, we lived with it.

Call after call, question after question, until I could almost answer every question by rote.

"Hello, Wynn residence... Yes, she is a vampire... Yes, she has fangs... two... Yes, I am positive... only two. One on each side of her mouth... No, she has never bitten any human and she only bites animals when she feeds on them... Yes, it has been thoroughly documented that she has never bitten any human, not even by accident... Yes, she fed off of the family dog because no cows were available... Absolutely not! She has never killed any dog or cow she has fed off of and she will not feed upon any animal if she senses that this would hurt it... No, it has been scientifically documented that the animals she has bitten have not turned into vampires, and none of the offspring of those animals have become vampires either... No, I am not a vampire... No, my parents are not vampires, nor are any of my family, relatives, or friends. Only my sister... Yes the FBI knows all about my sister and where she is at all times... Yes, twenty four hours a day... Yes, all of this information is available on the internet. The FDA's Department of Vampire Affairs can provide you with a listing of all legal, medical, scientific, and non scientific documentation... Thank you for calling..."

Therefore when the political firestorm erupted in early 2012, we had no choice but to change and the ones who insisted upon this change were the telephone company and the government.

Actually they begged us to switch to a different telephone system: "Calls to you are overloading the system! They have crashed the Northern Santa Barbara exchange four times in this week alone!"

That explained the momentary periods of peace and quiet we had been having for the past six months.

They then offered: "We will pay for and maintain it, free of charge! Forever!"

The changeover took place on February 29, 2012, and both the telephone company and government were lightning swift to announce our worldwide, toll free 800 number phone: VAMPIRE.

It formerly belonged to another business, probably X-rated, until the government acquired it and the former company was grateful.

They were tired of dealing with nonstop calls inquiring about real vampires and about us, and getting next to no sales in return for their time because their phone lines had been jammed the way our new one immediately was.

We in turn, were grateful because we now had far fewer phone calls to deal with, and Santa Barbara's north county phone lines no longer crashes because the toll free number routes these calls to somewhere that can handle the volume.

Probably Los Angeles, Phoenix, or Dallas, or maybe India, Mexico, or the Philippines.

The telephone's programmed message read: You have reached the home of the vampire, Julie Wynn. Due to the excessively high volume of calls we have been forced to install this automated system. Please utilize the menu to get the information you need.

For languages other than English, press 9.

To support the automobile dealership, press Star.

Professional and news media inquiries, press Pound.

For vampire anatomy, feeding, and behavior, press 1.

For vampire's human family's religion, press 2.

For unique vampire needs, including sunlight avoidance, press 3.

For the human response to vampire existence, press 4.

For facts about the vampire's human family, press 5.

For vampire facts and myths, press 6.

For internet and email addresses, press 7.

For the answering service, press 8.

Each topic also listed internet and email addresses, and what you got when you pushed the buttons were as follows.

The Star Key routed you to the dealership.

The Pound Key sent you to the universities who were studying Julie and us, and coordinating news media requests in conjunction with the Department of Vampire Affairs.

Numbers one through seven, routed you to recorded messages on the topics of your choice, and numbers one and two were the most popular by a wide margin, with six being a distant third.

We know this because the system tallied the number of calls.

Number six, vampire facts, was where we inserted details and facts that irritated and countered the fanatics.

One was the confirmation that Julie was born at nine in the morning.

Another is that she refuses to kiss, preferring to show her affections by humming.

Later, we learned that to her, the mouth is only for feeding and she is very protective of it, but even announcing this fact, plus the fact that she has never bitten anyone, not even a finger or hand, has not stopped some people from looking for bite marks on my family and on me. Even today. Especially on our necks.

When I am in a good mood, I wear a V-neck shirt or basketball jersey.

When my mood is foul, I wear the most massive long sleeve turtleneck I can buy.

By the way, the answering service was not our idea, or our doing.

It was a joint venture between the FDA, USDA, FBI, and the universities.

This allowed them to assess who was trying to reach us.

In exchange, graduate students in Public Relations, Psychology, Communications, Sociology, Criminology, Mathematics, Engineering, Computer Science, Statistical Analysis, and many more, now have plenty of data upon which to base research papers.

It probably got into numerous scientific journals too.

This setup also screened most of the nuisance calls, and all but a few of the serious threats, for which we were very grateful.

The latter was why the FBI wanted in, because it made tracking and dealing with those calls much easier, since 800 numbers always acquire the number from wherever a call is made.

The FBI said it was worth the price and naturally, the universities and the government screened our emails and handled the internet, which saved our lives because no person, family, or personal computer, can handle that volume of electronic morass.

This was confirmed when several graduate students attempted to implement a more personalized response system, and failed.

The reason for the failure was sheer volume.

Even the personnel already in place, were not enough, and the students concluded that about five hundred thousand people would be needed just to semi-personalize the emails alone.

Therefore, the mass input got mostly automated impersonalized responses, and we survived by dealing with the stuff they let through, and by having a private phone line and several unique email addresses that only a select few knew about.

This dampened the fire, but did not put it out, and the reason was public access. Our home address was no secret, and thanks to excessive news media coverage of vampire election year issues, and the fact that the economy was rebounding, people again felt comfortable traveling and many of them wanted to see the vampire.

This became more than just a problem.

It became a nightmare, for the incoming hordes were more than merely problematic.

The initial problem was that this residential area's streets were not designed to handle that much traffic or that many tourists.

Next came security headaches due to incoming fanatics and criminals, though years later, it was confirmed that hard-core criminals and gangs stayed away, since Santa Maria's FBI and police presence was more than just for show.

Finally, tourists need lodging and for California, the ultimate ongoing problem was and still is: Water.

Long before Julie was born, the State of California often struggled to deliver the volume of water that the central coast region needed.

Thus, the sudden influx strained the water system to the max.

The reason is that California is mostly arid, and global warming has upended the state's natural drought and rain cycles, yet even when it rains, the state's vast population and farms need that water.

Therefore, the initial solution was single day "afternoon fly-in, take a bus-ride, same night fly-out" tours, along with interviews of either us or our neighbors by prior arrangement.

This got us through June of 2012, when the rush began in earnest.

At that point the authorities had no choice but to impose visiting restrictions, which sort of helped, but not really.

One example was the car dealership, which was being overrun by those who only wanted to meet or interview my dad.

This made it impossible for dad and the dealership to conduct business, forcing him to take a leave of absence, which he grumbled about because he loves selling cars.

Thanks to medical research monies and cattle inspection fees, and later, the Street Legal War's legal settlements, money was no issue, but the horde then attempted to follow dad home.

The fact that he needed to be a night owl, so he could shepherd his daughter to ranches and elsewhere was deemed problematic by those who wanted full access to him at their convenience.

This mayhem forced the government to schedule a meeting and everyone from the neighborhood was there.

Security was no problem because California's governor had covertly mobilized the National Guard.

They protected the neighborhood and guarded our meeting place.

This alone confirmed how problematic the situation had become.

YOU SMELL LIKE THE DOG

The Wednesday evening July eleventh, meeting took place in the high school gym, which barely held all of the people who needed to be there. In addition to residents, federal, state, and local officials were there, as were the police, the National Guard, and reporters.

However this meeting was not broadcast live, enabling the editing or removal of information that would have adversely impacted us, the neighbors, the city, and whomever.

True to form, three year old Julie did what she thought was expected, pointing out those who were ill, including the memorable moment when she interrupted the man who owned the dog named Bruiser.

He had stepped up to the podium microphone to voice his view that: "The vampire family should leave and never come back."

He had been speaking for about a minute when Julie calmly, but loudly announced with the blunt candor of childish certainty: "You are very sick."

Those near enough to hear her words, chuckled, because her timing was accidentally perfect, but before the federal moderator could intervene, the man snapped: "I didn't ask for your opinion, you little bloodsucking monster!"

Mom snapped back: "Look at you! A grown man yelling at a child! She's only three, so she is most certainly not referring to your words! She is simply telling you as best she can, that you need to see a doctor as soon as possible."

Julie built on that: "You are very sick. You smell like the dog."

This sampling of three year old candor needed an explanation, which dad provided after the moderator restored order: "Three nights ago, Julie inspected a herd in San Luis Obispo.

"When the dog rushed out and barked at us, she told the rancher that his dog was very sick, even though it was young and looked perfectly healthy.

"The next evening, the researchers who are studying Julie's abilities, told us that three hours after we left, the dog died of a heart attack. So as much as I disagree with your views, sir, I suggest that as soon as you finish speaking, you get to the hospital... fast!"

"I don't believe that crap and you are still bloodsucking monsters!"

Because several television cameras now had me in their sights, with a big smile, I loudly countered: "Cowsuckers! Please!"

The crowd roared with laughter, and the man finished speaking, but he refused to go to the hospital despite assurances that the examination would be free. Besides, he had full medical insurance.

Instead, later that night, he died at home in his bathroom.

The cause was heart failure.

As for the meeting, all of the issues were documented.

These ranged from overcrowded streets and loss of parking, to littering and constant inquiries from tourists who wanted more than a bus tour. Hence our neighbors were being harassed because their homes were mistaken for the Wynn residence.

We, of course, suffered from these same trials and tribulations. Naturally, crime was a problem, but fanatics were deemed the worst of all, because they were forcing their views upon those who did not want to hear them, tourist and resident, and they were holding anti vampire protests that they had not gotten permits for.

These protests blocked sidewalks and sometimes streets, and were so disruptive that all of us were demanding a total end to them.

In fact, some who had formally been of the fanatic persuasion had seen the light, because incoming fanatics had threatened and harassed them, even as they repeatedly proclaimed agreement.

Thus they now knew how the rest of us felt and had become fanatic supporters of the neighborhood's anti fanatic movement.

As for solutions, some were humorous "if only we could!" like: "An amusement park designed so fanatics can live out their fantasies," and "Let Bruiser have at them. He'll gladly take them all out!"

Then came genuine solutions, like: "Seal off the neighborhood and have guarded gated entries," and "Build a castle just off of the freeway, complete with hotels, parking lots and signs saying: The Vampire Lives Here!"

Dad joked: "If the amusement park has trees, we could call it: Fangsylvania!"

Mom muttered under her breath, so low that I could barely hear her: "If they offer to move the dealership to that location, your father will likely vote for it…"

When the idea of having us relocate was suggested, Paul Gentry went to the podium and gave one of the most accurate insights of the evening: "Even if the Wynn family moves out of the state, that will not change the fact that Julie was born here… so tourists, opportunists, and fanatics will continue coming… now, and most likely for decades to come.

The only change will be the volume of traffic… maybe… and they will still come knocking on our doors. More than a few of them will continue attempting to use us and our neighborhood for publicity, proselytizing, and profiteering."

Equally valid was that overriding all solutions were two real world issues, one spoken, one unspoken.

The talked about issue was money because no matter what was decided, it was going to cost money.

Money that would have to come from somewhere.

The unspoken reality was that this was an election year, so no real solutions would be implemented until after the vote.

Reason: The vampire issue was the only genuine, yet safe debatable topic and neither side wanted to nullify it by solving it.

Also, money was too tight to spend on a project that might be canceled if a change in the Administration occurred.

For these reasons, a short term fix was recommended.

The plan was to partially seal off the neighborhood with temporary barricades and gated entries. It was not foolproof, but it was cheaper than hiring an additional hundred or more policemen, or calling in the National Guard for a long term stay.

Then, as the meeting came to a close, one of our nearer neighbors, Mr. Farnsworth, spoke: "My wife and I are lifelong Christians, so the issue of Christian fanaticism is as troubling to us, as is the fanaticism of foreigners who abuse their religion in precisely the same manner and for precisely the same reasons that Christian fanatics do... to accomplish their vile personal aims.

"Since fanatics have created organizations to proselytize their causes, like the Anti Vampire League, my wife and I have decided that we need to form an organization to publicize the fact that the majority of Christians are not fanatics.

"That the majority of Christians adore God and Jesus and obey His commandments because we love Him and we to want to obey them.

"Especially the commandments to love our neighbors, and to love our enemies too, and to leave the judgment solely to God and Jesus.

"Therefore, our goal is to become a voice to counter the howling done by the wolves in sheep's clothing. To counter the fanatics.

"To this end, we are founding the Christians Against Lunatic Fanatics Society, obviously nicknamed the CALF Society.

"We welcome those of like mind, Christian and Non Christian, to please join us in this endeavor. Thank you."

Mr. Farnsworth's proposal won unanimous applause and that same evening the CALF Society's first meeting was held and its charter was written.

This founding turned out to be far more important than any of us realized at the time, for CALF eventually became the central voice of opposition to religious, racial, and political fanaticism in this country.

CALF also worked with other faiths throughout the world, helping those people find methods for battling fanaticism in ways harmonious to their religions and beliefs.

Thus CALF and its later offshoots have done much to make the world a better and safer place for all of us.

Mr. and Mrs. Farnsworth, I thank you, and so does my family.

So do billions of people throughout the world.

Let it finally be noted that Julie was precisely like the other young children who were there.

Too young to know what was really going on, and too preoccupied with whatever caught her attention to do more than watch, listen, and occasionally tell someone that they were sick.

Thus it came to pass as I was carrying Julie out of the meeting, walking between our parents, that we saw the man who was Bruiser's owner, quite a ways in front of us, intent upon reaching his car quickly so he could leave sooner.

Julie was the one who called our attention to him. Pointing, she told us: "He is very sick. He is going home."

I wanted to know: "How do you know he is going home?"

"I smell it."

We conveyed her words to the researchers after we got home, and we were not the least bit surprised when the general details of his death were reported in the morning newspaper.

I FORGOT TO FACTOR IN PLANET X

Shortly after Julie turned three and a half, she became aware of the fact that revealing a fang or two, evoked reactions from those watching her.

Children were curious and sometimes shy, but the adults were all over the map, so like all young children, she tried many different things in an attempt to learn what the reactions would be.

This was when she discovered that grinning wide, then leaning forward, was not well received, but tilting her head to one side and revealing a fang or two, was considered cute.

So cute that by mid October, the Julie Vampire Doll, that mom and dad reviewed and approved, had become a best seller.

The sales line was a classic: "When she hums, she wants cows!"

If a child wanted one or more toy cows designed to feed this doll, they were extra and very popular too.

This doll set was the one Julie enjoyed most, since it was one of the few vampire toys she could identify with.

She named her doll "Alice Marie" after her friends Alice and Marie who attended Julie's evening preschool class.

This class was filled to capacity, for mothers who worked evenings loved it, but it had come into being because Julie's "allergy to sunlight" made her a child with special needs, so my parents had been told to enroll her in the county's Special Education program.

They did, whereupon an IFSP, the Individualized Family Service Plan for infants and preschoolers, was written, forcing officials from city, county, state, and federal agencies, to cow wrestle over how best to meet Julie's needs.

The vampire question added more cows and legal issues to the mix and these meetings became ample fodder for research papers.

The debate regarding whether integrating a vampire had to be done according to civil rights laws, or special education mandates, or both, was a classic.

It was finally resolved by a special act of Congress.

The Vampire Education Act of 2012.

Since the summer tourist rush was over, dad was able to return to the dealership and mom was grateful: "I love him dearly, but not in the house!"

This offhanded comment won knowing empathy from many wives, but bewildered their husbands, who did not understand what living with a restless caged tiger was like.

As mom privately noted: "Vampires are easier to live with. Just give them a cow or two and they are content to slink around the edges of a room in the hope of sneaking up on an alluring neck or two... and that's it!"

This pretty much summed things up because the real changes were the expected ones.

Julie loved preschool and enjoyed making new friends because she was indeed a sociable little girl who loved to talk and listen.

She enjoyed learning and already knew the shapes of letters correctly in a manner that was far beyond her age level.

Likely because she is so visually aware. In fact, the only things that bewilder her are those related solely to humans.

One example is the lifelong source of conflict between mom and Julie: Perfumes and fragrances.

Mom adores them and feels that they are the key to paradise on Earth. She has always made a point of having something fragrant in every room in the house. The stronger the better.

As for Julie, she came to despise them to a degree that is hard to explain, but is best described by the fact that by the time she was three and a half, if she was in a room when mom scented it, she angrily showed her fangs – never to bite – but apparently to her vampire way of thinking, showing fangs in this manner reveals how upset and furious she is.

It took mom a while to realize that the total absence of humming when fangs are shown in anger, means that Julie is as angry as it is possible to be, because hums of discomfort and displeasure are what normally accompany these sentiments.

Later, mom reckoned that vampires are hunters, so need to be fragrance free, and in this day and age, that may be asking the impossible.

Even so, Julie still persists in trying to find soaps, clothing, and other items that have no scents. This eventually became yet another avenue of scientific research, but cooking continues to mystify her because nothing else in nature needs to do it.

Julie knows that mom, dad, and I, do it, and that we eat what is cooked. She accepts this as part of life, but she does not really understand it, so back in 2012 when the girls and boys in preschool played cooking, Julie joined in, then later confronted mom: "Why?"

Mom had the ready answer: "We cannot eat like you do, so we do this instead."

That answer was sufficient enough for the three and a half year old, and events like these left us feeling that after the November elections, life would hopefully return to normal.

Of course, I should have known better since I was now thirteen and constantly wondering: "What's normal?"

Normal seemed to be returning when the fanatics asked everyone to boycott Halloween and in protest against the fanatics, millions of people who normally ignored it, gleefully participated.

Many dressed as vampires because vampires were even more in, than they had been last year.

So too were cows, but mom decided to dress Julie as a princess, since the idea is to dress as something you are not.

However, Julie was so into showing off her fangs that mom finally gave up and added a cape so Julie could be a princess-vampire.

Normal also seemed headed our way when the President was reelected by a landslide on November 6, 2012.

The fact that the most staunchly pro vampire candidates won the majority of the seats nationwide, was reassuring, even as pundits and commentators wondered whether the anti fanatic Halloween protest and the Julie Vampire Doll had anything to do with the increasingly pro vampire sentiments in this country.

Then came the other kind of normal.

On Thursday, November fifteenth, I was hastily jamming my breakfast dishes into the sink, belatedly thankful that they were plastic, not china, when mom, who was studying the astrological-numerological scratch notes she had just made, suddenly advised me: "Watch out for trouble today... likely heated. Mars has just gone into retrograde and it is big time in your house."

By that, she meant my astrological house and given that I was already a little late for school, I spoke on the run: "Mom... you know I am like way not into signs and numbers and things!"

"You should at least heed the warning when Mars goes into retrograde. Just keep your eyes and ears open for trouble and you will be fine. You're a Rabbit, so good fortune will find you if you let it."

The Chinese consider the year of the Rabbit to be the luckiest sign to be born under, while "retrograde" means that a planet looks like it is traveling backwards through the night sky.

Astrologers believe that whenever planets go backwards, bad things are supposed to occur.

However, given all that had happened since the world learned about Julie, I flippantly countered: "It is Earth that is in retrograde, so what's supposed to happen already?"

Mom, who had not once lifted her eyes from her notes, paused, looked at them with a head tilt, then decreed: "Too complex to calculate precisely. Probably means that unexpected visitors will show up today... looking for you."

"What is so unexpected about reporters, journalists, tourists, fanatics, dueling protesters, and the mail carrier?" I countered as I grabbed my book bag and flung open the front door.

I was interrupted in mid-stride by a policeman who was about to knock on our door.

To cover my bases and pretend that the officer was not really unexpected, I hastily added: "And the police. Mom... a policeman is here to see you."

Dad hollered from the bathroom: "I'll be right there!"

"Coming!" mom yelled as she ran to the door: "Drats! I forgot to factor in Planet X again!"

The policeman turned to me: "Son. I need to speak with you too."

Mom overheard his words and glanced at me, I pretended neutrality, and dad, his face half shaven, just showed up, calmly bracing for whatever was coming.

The officer kept it simple: "We have just received a bomb threat. School is being delayed until we finish searching the campus. The

FBI wants to check your house and yard, and the dealership too, just to be on the safe side. The bomb squad will be here shortly. I will wait in my car until they come, then verify them for you, since I have worked with these agents before."

Dad nodded, but otherwise kept his thoughts to himself.

Meanwhile, I was relieved because this gave me extra time to finish some homework I had said was done, but really was not, while mom spoke to no one in particular: "Now we know what can happen when Earth goes into retrograde."

"Not Planet X?" I inquired a little snidely.

"Unlikely. Given its current location, the only thing it would signify today, is the need to deal with unfinished tasks or something..."

I beat a hasty retreat and made a special effort not to let mom see me frantically finishing my homework.

As for the bomb threat, it turned out to be a hoax, but the search was not. Mom even had to go into the castle and wake Julie, so she would not be surprised when the FBI searched it.

After that part was over, mom sounded the alert: "Expect her to be hungrier than usual when she wakes up. She started humming when the bomb sniffing dog entered."

BACKWARDS LATIN

The bomb threat was the beginning of the end of our dream to stay where we were.

Dad said it best: "It does not bother me if some fanatic choses to damn his own soul by murdering me... but harming the neighbors and ruining their lives because I'm stubborn and hardheaded... is not something I want on my conscience."

I hated the thought of leaving my friends, especially Tom, but I felt the way dad did, for the one thing I did not want, was for Tom and his parents to be injured or killed by fanatics.

These sentiments and mom's agreement, paved the way for an early evening meeting on Friday, December 14, 2012, with Dr. Allen and several government officials, who offered several proposals.

First was a house on the ranch. I would be bussed to my current junior high school, Julie could continue going to her evening preschool, and linked to this proposal was the government's plan to build a castle on one of the hilltop ridges south of Orcutt, where Highway 101 begins heading down into the Santa Maria valley.

This castle's location would be easy to guard, since its only road would be to and from the freeway, and it would be used as a decoy.

We would spend most of our time in the house on the ranch and show up at the castle only enough to maintain the illusion.

It would also be distant enough from Santa Maria to reduce the tourist impact, yet close enough that those in the valley would still get tons of legitimate tourist business.

Another idea was to move to Pozo, just east of Santa Margarita, in San Luis Obispo County, since this northern region has cattle and Julie had already made numerous trips up there to inspect the herds.

Hence if we moved to Pozo, driving Julie to the many ranches up there, would be easier and the area would be reasonably easy for the government to guard because its few access roads are rural.

Then there was the option we had never imagined.

The island of Hawaii, the Big Island.

This was when we learned that Hawaii has several large cattle ranches and other things that make it very attractive to a vampire.

Deep caves in the island's hard volcanic rock would provide Julie with ideal protection from sunlight and since tourism has long been a major part of their economy, adding a vampire to the attractions list was something those on the Big Island and its largest city, Hilo, were more than willing to accommodate, for this idea had already been presented to them and discussed.

Better still, monitoring fanatics would be much easier and cheaper, because Hawaii is a distant island, hence easier for the government to guard and harder for fanatics to sneak into.

The only downside was that beyond Julie's herd and health assessments and the vampire studies for which all of us were being compensated, there might be little my parents could do in the way of work.

Dr. Allen countered: "Having all of you safe is more than just a priority. It is a victory against the fanatics, who in their arrogance and bigotry, would send us racing back to the dark ages."

Mom wondered: "If we leave, won't they think that they have chased us away or quarantined us on the island?"

"Not if we present it as a research endeavor which will require only a few years to complete. Its success will allow us to extend it if needed... and this is actually true. Hawaii's genetic isolation and the size of its ranches will allow us to do the kind of research and testing that cannot be done as well in this region.

"One example is an epidemiological study to see if diseases can be totally and completely eradicated by early detection or if new problems arise."

"It is a very tempting offer," dad confessed: "We just hate the idea of leaving family and friends behind…"

It was a hellish dilemma, but the only other options were to stay where we were or move to Pozo, then ride out the storm, or have the castle built and take our chances.

In the hope of staying, mom inquired: "Is there a way to build a house on the edge of town, with no other houses around it and a road that would deter those who do not know it?"

Dad groused: "Just don't call it: Serpentine Lane, or the fanatics will see it as a sign from God."

The FBI representative remarked: "Nothing is genuinely terrorist proof, but we can certainly assess it. Castle Road or something similar, would likely have to be its name… because a road is impossible to hide. Just keep in mind that even common names can be abused, and fanatics are masters at finding ways to abuse them."

Since this meeting occurred at our house, after awakening, Julie had entered the living room and was sitting on mom's lap.

Until now, she had been preoccupied with her doll, then she suddenly joined the conversation.

During story time, the preschool teacher had been reading about a girl who spared a dragon and became a knight.

Since part of this story took place in a castle, Julie now knew what a castle was and when the FBI representative offered his idea, she added hers: "Cow Castle Road."

She was saying it to herself, playing with the words, but we loved it and decided that if we needed to have a public road built, Cow Castle Road would be it.

The meeting ended on this note, and here it needs to be noted that in some respects, mom has always been a rebel.

She rarely argues, but neither does she back down, and like dad, she refuses to be intimidated.

The way she snapped at Bruiser's owner when he spoke rudely to her daughter, was typical.

So too is the fact that she adamantly insists upon walking whenever possible, rather than driving, and at stop signs and driveways, she lets cars go first: "My feet get better gas mileage than your car ever will!"

Thus, weather permitting, she walked Julie to preschool, usually accompanied by dad or neighborhood friends.

If my homework was not computer dependent, I sometimes went, for the large desks in the room next to the preschool, enabled me to spread my work in a manner better than our dining room table or the floor, neither of which were sister-proof.

Thus it came to pass that shortly after Cow Castle Road's name was created, Julie fed, then mom, dad, and I, walked her to school.

Since it was a typical December evening, it came early, and thanks to the vagaries of global warming, it was warmer than normal.

Thus the neighbors were out and about and so were tourists.

So too was a member of the fanatic persuasion.

I feel kind of dumb stating the obvious, but we were instantly recognized, delighting the tourists who could return home and rightly claim that they had seen the vampire.

The belated use of cameras lent credibility to their claims, adding dim flashes of light to our well lit residential neighborhood.

As for the fanatic, he did not say his name, nor did he provide any revealing information about himself or his church, but we saw him coming and mom lifted Julie into her arms.

As he walked towards us, the determined look on his face reminded me of a man struggling with constipation.

So too did the sound of his thundering voice: "Spawn of Satan! In the name of Christ Jesus, I command you to return to Hell!"

Three and a half year old Julie did not know what his words meant, but before mom, dad, or anyone else could intervene, the fanatic spewed forth in a language none of us had ever heard.

Nor had those in the surrounding crowd which continued to swell as neighbors protectively raced over, for the fanatic's manner and words had a threatening tone.

Also, there were probably some plainclothes police officers in the crowd and all of the tourists looked equally ready to protect us, since none of them shared that fanatic's beliefs.

Still, everyone stayed a little back, as mystified by the spewing gibberish as we were.

Finally, dad interrupted: "Sir. Can you explain in English, whatever it is that you are trying to say?"

The man rudely snapped: "None of your business!"

He then apparently resumed, using words that sounded even more nonsensical because in his haste to say them, they became so blurred, that it would have rendered any language incomprehensible.

Dad turned to his daughter: "Julie. Do you understand him?"

"No."

Her voice was so definitive that dad again interrupted: "As you have just heard... I asked my daughter if she understands what you are saying... and she said no. Therefore I must ask you to please speak English, or allow us to continue on our way."

All of us later admitted that the fanatic's answer was one we never anticipated: "All of the devil's children speak Backwards Latin and Backwards Greek, so she understands me perfectly!"

His statement prompted mom's stunned inquiry: "Backwards Latin? Backwards Greek? Ah... what are they?"

One of our neighbors wanted the answer too: "Sir. In high school and college, I studied Latin and Greek and what you are speaking comes nowhere close to those languages... or any of the others that I know... so please explain."

Irritated over being interrupted, the fanatic snapped: "It's Latin and Greek spoken backwards in the foul perverted manner that only Satan's minions can do!"

Dad calmly pounced: "Sir. You claim to speak these languages and you have just stated that only Satan's minions can speak them. Does this mean that you are one of Satan's minions?"

Some in the crowd chuckled and in fury, the fanatic angrily yelled: "I am not Satan's servant! I serve only God and Jesus!"

From his jacket pocket, he rapidly pulled out an unexpectedly large silver cross, then bellowed: "Fiend of Hell! Behold the wrath of God!"

Thrusting the cross towards Julie so its front was fully visible to the young vampire, he yelled: "In the name of Jesus Christ, I command you, Spawn of Satan! Demon of Hell! Depart immediately to the deepest depths of Hell!"

Though Julie did not like the sound of his voice, she felt safe in mom's arms and naturally, she still had absolutely no clue as to what he was saying.

Instead, her words were those of any young child who thinks she is being offered something: "Pretty! I want it!"

She reached for the cross, obviously to take it.

In belated haste the fanatic yanked it away, bewildered because Julie was definitely not cringing.

After a moment, he inquired in a demanding, insulting voice: "Fiend of Hell! Have you never seen the Cross of Jesus?"

Dad ignored the insult and calmly noted: "We have one in every room in our house... including the room where she sleeps... and I agree with my daughter. The one you are holding is beautiful."

The man froze, then demanded: "Do you confess that Jesus Christ is the Son of God?"

Mom stepped in: "Of course He is! The Holy Bible states in the Book of John, chapter one, verse three: 'All things were made by him; and without him was not any thing made that was made.' Therefore, He alone created all of us... including Julie!"

In response, the man imperiously decreed: "Unclean things cannot understand the Word of God! ...or the ways of God!"

Mom never cared for the selective literalness used by fanatics to twist and manipulate the Bible's words for their own personal ends.

Her voice was calm, but unyielding: "Then please explain how taking a bath will make your blasphemous denial of God's written word, more understandable to any of us?"

In fury, the fanatic departed, and the crowd's applause revealed how deeply our sentiments were shared.

WORSER THAN A SICK DOG

The neighborly support we had just received made it harder to leave, but it was Tom's parents who gave us the needed rationales when we shared the Backwards Latin story with them.

We went to their house immediately after Julie's preschool class, and Paul came straight to the heart of the matter: "This is a battle the neighbors are willing to fight, but many years of this will probably be more than they can stomach.

"Besides, no matter what their religion, fanatics create theological loopholes so they can deceive themselves into believing that it is lawful to do the very evils that are totally, completely, and explicitly forbidden by their scripture's uncompromising commandments."

There was no need to say more, for even I knew that he was referring to death threats and murder. The satanic actions all fanatics adore, conveniently forgetting that obedience to scriptural commandments to never hate and never kill, are mandated for all believers and that lip-serving religion counts for nothing.

However, what surprised us was that Susan and Paul knew all about Backwards Greek and Backwards Latin.

When I asked how they knew about them, Paul sighed: "When you are on the wrong end of a loaded cross, wielded by a potentially violent madman, it helps to know what he might be trying to say or what he intends to do."

We all wanted to know: "What are they?"

Susan shared: "There are many variants. The most common is to read the words from back to front. 'Please come home' then becomes 'Home come please' which is the favorite because it is the easiest.

"Another major variant is to change the words to their opposite or to something profane, so the meaning changes from 'Please come home' to 'Please leave home' or something vile.

"The final major variant which your telling implies was the one used, is to read the letters backwards, so 'Please come home' becomes 'Esaelp emoc emoh' ...or 'Emoh emoc esaelp' if they read the sentence backwards too."

Paul explained: "Some people believe that since the devil is supposed to corrupt everything, he will corrupt the holy scriptures too. Reading things backwards has long been believed to be one way of doing this."

Dad grinned: "What about Backwards English?"

Mom built on Paul's explanation: "Of course, it never occurs to them that Satan would insidiously guide them to find theological excuses that completes and perfects the perversion of their beliefs, so that their words and deeds worship and serve the antichrist."

Paul mused: "Along with politics, that sounds like the ultimate definition of Backwards English."

Susan agreed: "That is precisely why fanatics so willingly serve the terrorist cause, isn't it?"

This confirmed that nothing was going to change, so dad told them the options we had been given, giving rise to Susan's confession: "I love the idea of your staying close, because we are going to miss you... a lot... but the farther away you are publicly documented to be, the sooner most of them will lose interest in coming here."

We smiled at the unspoken joke, knowing that few in this world would consider Santa Maria the ultimate vacation spot, yet her words rightly implied that even Pozo would be too close.

That fanatics would continue to plague Santa Maria if we only moved a short distance way.

For these reasons we chose Hawaii with the understanding that our Santa Maria home would be maintained so we would have a place to stay when we returned for occasional visits.

This was more than agreeable, for as the FBI representative explained: "We do not dare let anyone live in your house or sell it, because it was the home you lived in when Julie was born. Even after you leave, some fanatic is probably going to want to make name for himself by destroying it."

Thus the move was planned for the beginning of January, giving us time to visit with family and friends before leaving.

Neither our plans, nor the dates, were revealed due to concern that this announcement might impel the fanatics to come after us while we were still easier, more convenient targets.

This withholding turned out to be unnecessary because the fanatics were already gunning for us.

As mom publicly noted afterwards: "They wanted murder and destruction to be their Christmas present to Satan."

Dad added: "Doing it in the name of Jesus Christ is the ultimate gift they can give the antichrist, isn't it?"

The attack occurred on Friday, December twenty first, but I need to begin with a not so brief explanation.

About two thousand years ago, the Mayans predicted that "this age" would end on December 21, 2012.

Physically, of course, the Earth continues to exist.

On the other hand, they were absolutely correct because this was when all of the world's nations took the first major steps that will soon put an end to the old way of doing things.

The man partly responsible for some of these changes, was the newly reelected President of the United States.

Since he was in his final term in office, he no longer needed to answer to anybody, freeing him to turn to the wealthy and corporate elite, and tell them: "You have only two choices. Accept the changes and adapt... or fight them and hope that the angry mobs only torture you to death."

As you know, he was correct because thanks to the GMO crisis, even in the smallest and most remote nations on Earth, anti corporate and anti exploitation sentiments were more than just at an all time high. They were finally exploding.

The anti economic slavery movement was on the verge of becoming fanatically rampant in every nation in the world and the only real laggard was the United States.

Yet even here, the slightest political misstep would have sent the government toppling with angry mobs seeking out the wealthy and their political and corporate henchmen for the kind of vengeance none wanted to endure.

This worldwide sentiment assured that there would be no place to escape to. Not even a tiny remote island on which to live in comfort for the remainder of one's days.

Since the handwriting was on the wall, the President got his way.

On the morning of December twenty first, he signed the Equal Rights Law, which contained a provision allowing it to be ratified by the States.

Thus it was also a Constitutional Amendment.

It granted genuine equal rights to all, including Julie, and one of those rights eliminated medical insurance in favor of having all medical services paid for by the government.

Thus instead of hundreds of billions of dollars going into the personal pockets of the wealthy elite who owned the insurance companies, with only a few billion in medical payouts being returned, the only expenses now, were the actual medical costs.

Thus even with taxes, ordinary people had far more spending money because all of the excessive insurance premiums, copays, and share of cost payments, were no more, while those who formerly worked in the many separate corporate insurance bureaucracies, were given retraining so they could acquire meaningful jobs.

Reason: Only one government agency now handles all medical payments, from infants to the most aged seniors, and its only job is track and pay genuine medical bills. Not to deny coverage.

People like grandma and grandpa Lee, who thoroughly understood the medical side of things, were asked to aid the government in this transition, so overnight, they became federal employees.

In addition, corporate profits were now limited by law which made everything except specialty items, very affordable.

One medical example was hearing aids, which had been manufactured for well under fifty "real world" dollars apiece, then sold by the corporations for up to five thousand dollars each, and most people who suffer from hearing loss need two, one for each ear.

Just like most sight problems need glasses, not monocles.

Grandpa Wynn, who had worn hearing aids since losing some of his hearing due to loud music, had long bitched: "The reason good hearing aids are expensive, is because politicians, advertisers, and commentators, do not want you to hear what they are really saying!"

Well this and many other things had just changed, like executive pay which shrank from obscene, down to reasonable.

On the other hand, those who did the real work, from audiologists, speech therapists, O&M instructors, teachers, and doctors, to factory workers, secretaries, common laborers, nurses, store clerks, farmers and farm workers, ranchers and cowboys, stock clerks, police, fire fighters, paramedics, chefs and cooks, janitors, machine operators, those in construction, and all other jobs, rural and city, were finally genuinely compensated for their labors.

They all received significant pay raises and since everyone in the United States and throughout the world now had spending money, the economy roared back to life.

Concurrently, a number of government, corporate, and wealthy individuals, including some from the United States, now had formal international arrest warrants outstanding for crimes ranging from war crimes and human rights violations, to environmental destruction and economic terrorism, including deliberate bank and stock market "failures" solely for the sake of their secret personal enrichment.

Failure to arrest them would have resulted in the kind of worldwide retaliation that even the United States and China together could not have withstood for long, and this same "fix it now or else" was true for global warming, oceanic rising, economic slavery and all other forms of slavery too, undoing pollution and environmental damage, along with genuine equal rights including to food and water, and more.

Of course many of these changes are still coming into being because they are so vast in scope.

On the other hand, some changes came lightening fast.

The world was swift to adopt a calendar change that made night shifts and chronicling the vampire's life, far easier.

Instead of ending each day a midnight, six o'clock in the morning is when the date changes and those who begin working before six, simply use the new day for all of their record keeping.

Also eliminated by popular vote was Daylight Savings Time.

Instead, clocks were set to Standard Time, then all time zones were moved up by half an hour, splitting the difference, ending the issue.

Now, the reason for even mentioning all of the things that you already know, is because all of these laws were more than just unpopular with fanatics.

Equality, equal rights, equal pay, and especially equal respect for all, infuriates fanatics because they are elitists who believe that they are the only ones entitled to rights, privileges, benefits, and respect.

They also believe that they alone have the right to tell the rest of us what we can and cannot do.

However, they were even more distressed by the dating and time changes because these implied that the masses of humanity were preparing to live in peace with the world's one and only vampire, in a manner would make everyone's lives easier and nicer.

Hence some fanatics considered these changes to be a satanic victory of epic proportions. They loudly decreed that the calendar and time changes were proof that the devil was remaking the world to better suit his plans for world domination.

Therefore when these changes were signed into law, the match was still too close to the powder keg for comfort.

The ones who wanted to blow it all to hell, were the fanatics.

Since so many holidays and family gatherings occur during the Christmas season, preschool was closed, enabling us to attend a Friday evening church service on the twenty first.

The service for young children enabled Julie to gleefully proclaim: "Jesus born with cows and sheeps!"

Given that she was three, this was a very acceptable introduction to our faith and it led to an after church Julie request: "I want sheeps please."

My parents reckoned that the researchers would be delighted, for until this moment, Julie had only wanted cows.

I sighed: "Sheepsucker and Lambsucker, just don't cut it!"

Dad countered with a grin: "Where's the beef?"

Then the fanatics approached.

This time there were six of them, including the Backwards Latin speaker who had accosted us back on December fourteenth, and we were grateful that there were far more plain clothed police and FBI special agents nearby, posing as tourists and residents.

Their increased presence was easily explained.

The first encounter had been reported and that same evening, the FBI had asked us to alert them prior to our outings, thus giving them the time they needed to be there in sufficient numbers.

The hope was that future fanatic encounters would be limited to just talk, and the six fanatics initially obliged, though unexpectedly, the targets were mom and dad who were royally preached at.

Finally, mom quietly exploded: "Please define belief."

"Gladly!" one decreed: "Belief means to believe in God!"

Another added: "Belief means to accept Jesus Christ and to proclaim that He is the Son of God!"

A third said: "To believe the Truth as proclaimed in the Holy Bible!"

Mom countered: "You are telling us what you believe in... but you are not even close to giving us a definition of the word, belief."

Dad knew where mom was heading: "How can you call yourselves believers in Christ and not know the meaning of the word, belief?"

"We know what the word belief means!"

"Then please define it."

"It means to have faith in God and..."

Dad was uncompromising: "That is another example of what you believe in. Why can't you define the word belief? After all... this word is clearly explained in the Holy Bible."

When they hesitated, mom pointed out that in First Corinthians, chapter thirteen, the Apostle Paul defines just how incomplete his own knowledge is, and therefore, how incomplete our knowledge is.

The fact that we only understand "in part," and "we see through a glass, darkly" and this lack of knowledge extends to prophesy, for the most that even the Apostles can do, is "prophesy in part,"

Dad reminded them that this limitation is precisely why the Holy Bible repeatedly reminds us to be humble believers, because our knowledge is incomplete.

He then restated mom's point: "Belief means to know only in part... not fully... and even the Apostles, let alone mere believers, do not know where the knowledge gaps in their beliefs actually are."

Still, the fanatics persisted in their self righteousness: "The Holy Spirit guides us perfectly!"

Mom noted: "The guidance is perfect but your lack of ability to understand it, is also confirmed by First Corinthians."

Then she quoted the first part of verse eleven: "When I was a child, I spake as a child, I understood as a child, I thought as a child..."

Having said this, she exploded: "Your refusal to humble yourselves before God and Jesus and admit that when it comes to God's Word and the Holy Spirit... your understanding is limited and incomplete... implies that you are Christian Pharisees! Your refusal implies that your only desire is to twist the word of God and blaspheme the Holy Spirit to accomplish your own personal ends!"

I jumped in: "That's what Jesus says Pharisees do!"

"We are not twisting the Holy Word of God!"

Mom thundered: "Then prove it! Stop harassing us and stop harassing everybody else! Stop accusing my child of being Satan's creation, because... Satan... cannot... create... anything... at... all! Only God can do that!"

"Satan corrupts God's creation!"

"He does indeed!" dad retorted: "Through lies and through twisting Scripture like he did when he tempted Jesus in the desert... and like he has been doing ever since... so the question is: Why won't you defy Satan by obeying the commandments that God and Jesus gave to all of us?

"Harassment glorifies Satan. Judging others glorifies Satan. Lying glorifies Satan. Hating your enemies glorifies Satan, and in case you have forgotten the commandments as explained by Jesus Christ Himself in His Sermon on the Mount... anger, hatred, and killing, all glorify Satan... so please stop now! Go home and leave all of us alone. In the name of our Lord, Jesus Christ, I ask this."

This blistering Bible centered counterattack momentarily stopped the fanatics in their tracks, because they were confronted with the growing realization that they could not preach that their beliefs were "the only true beliefs."

That claim would be an outright lie because even they had to admit to being mere believers. That is, people who had to hope that their beliefs might be right, because they actually genuinely do not know.

Therefore all of their arrogant proclamations of "exclusive insights and Holy Spirit knowledge" and their decree it they believed in "The Truth" was totally undercut by the reality of their own ignorance.

This also undercut their ability to legitimately utilize the Holy Bible to justify and sanction their hate, since that too was belief based.

By this time, all of us, family, neighbors, bystanders, police, and FBI agents, were hoping and praying that these fanatics would accept the fact that Jesus Christ and the Apostle Paul were absolutely correct about the limits of belief.

That Jesus Christ and the Apostle Paul were absolutely correct about the need for believers to humble themselves before God and their fellow men and women, and that the best thing they could do was to leave immediately, and not come back.

Unfortunately like all Pharisees, ancient and modern, these men were too self righteous and hard hearted to heed the words of the Holy Scripture they loudly claimed that they believed and obeyed.

Instead, they verbally pounced on Julie, demanding that she renounce Satan and confess that Jesus was the Son of God.

Mom countered again. The protective thunder in her voice was uncompromising: "She is only three! Tonight she was finally old enough to begin learning that Jesus was placed in a manger because there was no room at the inn... and like all children her age, all she really understands is that cows and sheep were there too!"

Huddling in the safety of mom's arms, Julie offered her assessment: "Nice cows. Nice sheeps."

Just then, the Backwards Latin fanatic pulled out his large silver cross and stepped forward.

Thrusting it within easy reach of my sister, he self righteously decreed: "She can prove her acceptance by holding or touching this cross. If she is too young to do so without help, you can place her hand upon it. If she can do so and live, that will prove that she is not the Spawn of Satan!"

Dad snapped: "You are not the determiner of her standing in God's eyes! Nor how its determined! ...and we are not subject to you at all, Mr. Christian Pharisee Tyrant! ...or to your church or your..."

What caused dad to pause, was Julie's reaction.

She buried her head in mom's shoulder, then protested: "It stink worser than a sick dog!"

Not trusting the man's motives, mom defended her daughter: "Why didn't you offer this the first time we spoke?"

Building upon Julie's revelation, she demanded to know: "Is it now covered with poison?"

Suddenly, the fanatic lunged, grabbing for Julie's arm.

In panic, mom twisted away and jumped back.

Dad immediately jumped in to shield his wife and daughter, but far faster were the three FBI agents who tackled the fanatic, and since the other fanatics attempted to attack, plainclothes police officers and FBI agents wrestled them to the ground as well.

Concurrently, as the Backwards Latin fanatic was being tackled, his face touched the cross and within seconds, he showed signs of being poisoned, for with the sole exception of its base, his cross was coated with a fast acting contact poison.

A poison transmitted through the skin.

He was rushed to the hospital and barely survived, but the fanatics' "Christian" claim was now "a proven lie" for their goal all along, had been to murder Julie in a covert and deceitful manner, which they intended to use to falsely proclaim: "God was the one who struck her dead."Obviously, the means that they used revealed their true values and beliefs. So too did their actions,

Equally obvious was that if mom, dad, or I, or the police or FBI agents, or any of the neighbors or tourists, had touched the cross and died, those deaths would have been totally acceptable to them and everyone in the entire world, knew it.

A WEREWOLF WOULD HAVE
MADE LIFE INTERESTING

Now you know why I am so anti fanatic.

To them, the murder of innocent bystanders is totally acceptable, so to protect those we love and innocent bystanders too, we had to move away from the city that was our home.

This brings me to the final relevant statements on this subject as it relates to Julie and my family.

Most fanatics are swift to admit that their religion commands them to not judge others, yet they find every excuse in the book to be judgmental, and more often than not, racist too.

I know this, because of the words and accusations that the fanatics continue heaping upon me and my parents, due to who my sister is.

Even after all of these years.

The vile words they use are appalling, but what they say about my sister is worse, so if you are into horror pornography just listen to their fantasies. They are so foul that none of them are clean enough to even be rated X.

That is why none are included in this book.

Not even the porn industry at its height, ever sank that low!

This is why I avoid having anything to do with those who use religion and belief to justify hate and bigotry so they can commit evil under the false pretense of ending it.

Their ultimate perversion is that they justify their right to commit evil by claiming that they are doing it in the name of God and righteousness, and I am as sick of that satanic excuse, as I am of them.

As for Hawaii, it gave my sister and our family, and the doctors and researchers, the safety, peace, and quiet, needed to live normal lives, because the fanatics were not done with Santa Maria just yet.

On the evening of July 2, 2013, bomb blasts destroyed two houses in the Santa Maria area.

The Wynn and the Gentry homes were destroyed and neighboring homes were damaged because fanatics do not care who they hurt.

Thankfully no one was seriously injured and the Gentry's decision to go to Tuesday evening Bible Study, saved them.

By the way, that church's Sunday school was where Tom and I first met when we were three, and where we became friends.

Anyway, two out of State fanatics, both white, confessed that they committed the bombings because the Gentry family is black.

As for my family's house, they bombed it because: "The vampire lived there" and they also bombed it in retaliation for the filming and publicizing the two fanatic encounters detailed in this book.

For fanatics, having the truth revealed is always unacceptable.

However, they did reveal lots of made-up belief based fantasies linking our two families to plagues and pestilences that will supposedly infect white people with vampires.

Apparently, they believe that vampires are an infectious disease. Really?

As everyone knows, those kind of rationales are so "typical of fanatics" that a slang word has come into being to describe their foul outputs: "Flop" – Fanatic Loony Poop.

Of course, no one is buying their excuses anymore, so the fanatics were sentenced to life in prison and sent to Guantánamo.

The Cubans now run that prison, which has become the jail that houses the entire world's war crimes criminals: Political, corporate, and the wealthy elites whom they loyally served.

Those criminals share one thing in common with the violent fanatics who have been sent there from every nation on Earth.

All of them want to infect the world with hate, violence, and murder, for the sake of their beliefs and even more, for the sake of their own personal gratification and enrichment.

These greed based satanic values made all of them the actual terrorists of this world.

On the positive side, thanks to worldwide donations, the Santa Maria homes were swiftly rebuilt, but Paul and Susan made a point of suing the fanatics and those who had supported and incited them.

So too did the government, and there were additional arrests for aiding and abetting, and for conspiracy too.

Those legal successes gave Tom the money that covered his university and medical school expenses.

He is now a Doctor of Osteopathic Medicine, a DO, and I can happily state for the record that Tom and I are best friends for life.

Whenever we are together, the magic returns, but when we are apart, we are able to go our separate ways secure in the deep bond of friendship.

As for me, I must have been totally corrupted by "the black influence" because I studied electronics and the required medical courses so I could follow in Paul Gentry's footsteps and become a BMET.

By the way, the filming of the two encounters we were bombed for, was not our doing.

Unbeknownst to us, though we should have been expecting it, was that every time we went out, the FBI recorded it so that if something happened, they would have irrefutable documentation.

This is why I can state that the public events I have written about, happened precisely that way, and in the case of the two fanatic encounters of the unwanted kind, the President and his advisors reviewed them, then asked my parents for permission to air them as part of the first genuine anti terrorist, anti hate campaign in United States history.

The CALF Society also uses them and the fact that these were aired worldwide, helped there too, for many living in lands where their own fanatics were just as locoweed as ours, used translations of mom and dad's countering arguments as springboards for their own.

This did much to foster the anti fanatic movement, as did the Santa Maria bombings, and this movement's most lasting legacy is the worldwide enactment of a Free Speech Law that has only three restrictions.

First: Speech becomes a crime when it is used to harm or incite harm against any living being, human and non human.

Second: Speech for the purpose of personal gain at the expense of others, be it economic, political, religious, or whatever, is a crime.

Third: Beliefs and opinions cannot be presented as facts unless factual documentation is presented that cannot be countered by other factual documentation.

Therefore, if one "set of facts" are being presented, so too must all other facts, so everyone can learn all viewpoints.

Included in the Free Speech Law is a provision acknowledging the right to believe anything as long as the first two provisions are not violated.

Belief based teachings and documents, including religious writings and videos, are now lawfully decreed to be Belief Based Speech.

Of course this law did not put an end to the hateful fanatics.

For some reason, they cannot accept the fact that God has done things in accordance with His Divine Will, rather than being obedient to their specific beliefs.

Even now, they claim that Julie is the work of Satan.

They even more loudly proclaim that "the creation of creatures of evil" in the form of "a single vampire" is "absolute proof" that this is the time of the antichrist.

Some of them even claim that Julie is the antichrist, conveniently ignoring biblical proclamations that Satan and his highest ranking spokesmen and henchmen, are males.

Thankfully, nowadays, few people agree with the fanatics, and the number of fanatics and their supporters are shrinking.

I believe this is proof that humanity is changing for the better now that economic slavery has been abolished worldwide.

Of course, what you want to know is the Julie story.

In response to the assassination attempt, we moved to Hawaii on December 27, 2012, instead of on January 6, 2013, which mom said was better, since January's numbers and stars turned out to be not quite as good.

Due to the moving upheaval, the sheep Julie wanted to try were postponed until after we settled into our new home outside of Hilo.

Due also to the ongoing existence of fanatics, few though they now are, the exact location must be kept secret since this is where my sister will likely spend most of her life.

However, the official street name is Cow Castle Road.

On the science side, the move to Hawaii gave the researchers more time to select the sheep they needed Julie to bite.

These were shipped to the island, then quarantined, so it was not until April 9, 2013, that the four year old got her wish.

Let it now be said that when Julie encountered her first ewe, mom, dad, and I, finally understood why young vampires feel such an intense need to play Chomp Neck.

Since this was only supposed to be an introduction, no one expected her to feed, so the ewe had not been hobbled or tethered.

Therefore, Julie had to catch it and she did, but even in the dimly lit corral, it was challenging because the ewe was fidgety and had room to run.

Thus Julie's Chomp Neck skills enabled her to put a far swifter end to the chase.

Then she fed and proclaimed as if she was stating the obvious: "Sheep are good. Cows are better!"

In response, dad joked: "So much for an extended stay in New Zealand..."

Mom took his island remark literally: "There is always Scotland, and Japan has beef that is world renowned for its flavor... so they will probably want to see what her bites do for their animals too."

Her remarks were based on the fact that back on April 6, 2013, the FDA and the USDA had announced the results of their testing.

Meats from the animals Julie fed upon, were deemed superior due to their flavor and due to the fact people with asthma, arthritis, and other inflammatory diseases, experienced improvements in their health after eating them.

Better still was that these traits appeared to be passed down from one generation to the next.

At the time, that possibility was going to take years and a lot of cows to confirm, but this did not stop the government from issuing two new meat labels.

The first was Paul's long envisioned: "USDA Certified Vampire Bitten," complete with two fangs in place of the double "t's" because there is no simpler way to say it.

The other label with fangs was: "USDA Certified Offspring From Vampire Bitten Animals."

Yet the real news was that the FDA finally had answers.

By themselves, her bites are meaningless, but combining her saliva with blood plasma produces a healing response that stops pain and seals bite wounds, while triggering an anti-inflammatory response that spreads throughout the body at speeds that scientists still cannot explain, thought the documentation of this speed is now ancient history.

Thus, thanks to Julie and the farsightedness of the Administration to protect her, cures for the above mentioned diseases and more, are now here, or on the near horizon.

So too are Scent Detection Monitors that spot illnesses and just as important are potent new pain-blocking drugs like Vampirdine, that have no side effects.

Finally, the fact that Tiny lived to enjoy his twenty second birthday, having died of old age, pain free thanks to sister's occasional bites, is more than newsworthy.

Since dogs his size usually live only half this long with the kind of good health and vitality he enjoyed to the end, everyone is excited and this area of research is being avidly pursued.

Finally, what I can say now, in 2029, is that the Certified Offspring label is only good for two generations.

Therefore, if we want exceptionally flavorful, good for human health meat, then we will have to live with the vampire and hope she breeds true when she finally has children.

Given her unique internal female anatomy, things could become interesting because MRI and ultrasound reveal that she is different in a way that no one yet understands.

Even so, the medical decree is that things should work.

That is, in terms of having babies.

As for Julie, she is a shy but outgoing young vampire who considers Hawaii her home, because the Big Island is what she remembers most, and where her family and friends are.

For her, Santa Maria smells very familiar when we visit, and she likes it a lot, but she prefers staying put.

She does not care for traveling, probably due to the noise.

On the other hand, she is only twenty and she is totally focused upon her academic studies at the University of Hawaii's Hilo campus.

Her major is Agriculture with the emphasis on ranching.

She has also grown up to be the kind of attractive that is only surprising because the boys are not as interested as they normally would be.

Of course, I understand their reasons, and even having movie star white teeth won't aid this cause.

Then again, maybe it will, because life naturally has its moments.

One of my favorite moments occurred two years after we moved to Hawaii, when a reporter who was interviewing dad, noted: "Recently, some fanatics have been attempting to incite concern by calling Julie a menace. They are saying… quote: 'She's gonna grow up to be a bloodsucker!' end of quote… What is your response?"

Having had several years to reflect upon this issue, dad was more than ready: "The word bloodsucker has a negative connotation, implying that someone is taking advantage of a situation.

"This describes precisely what those fanatics are attempting to do.

"They want to use Julie to incite others in a manner that will enable them to take advantage of that response, for reasons known only to themselves. This makes them the actual bloodsuckers, does it not?"

Dad then added: "To show the lunacy of their claim regarding what they think Julie is going to grow up to be… please remember… Julie can never be transformed into a vampire sometime in the future… because she already is one.

"She has been a vampire since the day she was born."

Max right!

Much to dad's disappointment, he could not go back to selling cars, so he obtained an advanced degree in English from the university. Then he acquired a teaching credential and now teaches in a local school.

The kids call him: "The Big Vampire."

I too have had my share of giving and taking these kind of jokes and dad made a point of once teasing me: "When Julie turns five, your mom and I might try for a werewolf!"

That I could handle: "Great! Julie can eat in the house once a month!"

Much later, dad admitted: "The government wanted us to see if we could duplicate Julie by having another child, but mom said it was not in the stars or the numbers. Soon thereafter, medical exams confirmed that having a third child would be medically dangerous for her, so we did not."

Too bad. A werewolf would have made life interesting.

Of course some things were predictable.

Whenever Julie saw a dog and began humming, we headed for the nearest cow, and though she enjoys clothing, even now, she really does not understand "the need" for it.

Especially coats and sweaters.

For a while, getting her to wear shoes was a challenge because they squeak. Even the ones we cannot hear, make sounds that she finds annoying, so the government has been trying to discover how to make silent shoes.

Even so, I tease them: "What next? Vampire Mary Janes? Fang Tipped Toes with Nightwalker heels? Ballerina Cow Stalkers?"

Then again, this is an endeavor neither they, nor we, ever envisioned Julie fostering, while the one we expected to see happen, never came to pass.

Sports.

Since Julie is so physically gifted, the schools she attended, wanted to shift some of their sports programs to late in the evening and let her be the superstar she is, by virtue of being a vampire.

In panic, the other schools countered that this would be unfair competition and refused to schedule anything except daytime events, which would have made for some interesting legal battles except that Julie has her own agenda.

Mostly ranchland jaunts, stalking cattle and perfecting her Chomp Neck skills.

To quote her: "I love being a free range vampire!"

This is an opening a brother can run with: "A USDA Certified Free Range Vampire!"

"Cram it, Leo! Go eat a cow!"

"Gladly! Well done, please!"

"Cook it yourself!"

"No choice, Julie... you can't!"

"Thank God!"

Anyway, being a free range vampire appeals to her sensibilities far more than does doing things with a ball, though she enjoys an occasional game of catch using a baseball.

A hardball that is.

One of her favorite games is to throw a baseball as far as she can into a field, then see how quickly she can find it, using mostly her sense of smell, because she has flung it so far.

Thankfully, no cows have been nailed to date, but she has come close a few times when the wind caught the ball and it accidentally sailed over a far distant hill into areas where cows were grazing.

Naturally she still loves sitting on a beach, enjoying the sand and the waves.

On the bemusing side, Julie hates Dracula with a passion.

She considers him to be a neurotic creature, actually "a creature that only a human would even think to create," who should have stuck to cows, or at least men.

Her reasoning, which is pure vampire, is that men are bigger, so have more blood. This allows her to decree that one reason Dracula was not thinking clearly, was because he was not eating enough.

Nor was he eating properly, at least from her perspective since she deems human blood "non-nutritious to the max!"

The tone in her voice confirms that she is indeed capable of feeling and expressing contempt.

She has also made it crystal clear to everyone in our family, that when it comes to sibling rivalry, she has the teeth for it: "Leo! Human blood smells horrid... but yours really stinks!"

The need to verify my health thwarts immediate counterattack and all of us know it, so the only thing I can belatedly say is: "Thanks a lot, fang face!"

"Anytime!" comes the grinning cheery reply, fangs and all.

Perhaps here would be a good time to note that Julie only bites the animals she feeds upon and she generally cooperates when medical researchers ask her to bite something.

But not always.

She has staunchly refused to bite humans, even for research purposes, and she wants nothing to do with human blood. Ever!

I love the words she used to protest the proposed "bite the human" research: "What are you trying to do? Make me sick?"

This refusal also keeps sibling rivalry from entering uncharted waters, so from the vampire perspective, my neck is still virginal.

On the other hand, thanks to our shared childhood, my neck is still fair game, as I learned several nights ago when Julie stopped by to visit, then surprised me with an unannounced game of Chomp Neck.

Naturally with me on the receiving end.

She claimed it was for old time's sake.

Right.

I suppose I should mention that whenever an obnoxious dog crosses Julie's path, she has no objections to teaching it manners by snacking on it.

After all, she is a vampire.

She is also as famous as anyone on Earth can be.

Her pictures are as well known, as are the promotional videos she stared in as a child and as a teenager, for the worldwide dental campaign to promote flossing and brushing.

It worked big time.

"Show off your fangs!" and "Reveal a fang or two!" became popular slogans and though I hate to admit it, my sister is a master when it comes to showing them off.

When Julie became a teenager, she decided that her fangs are sexy, but the young men I have spoken with, think otherwise.

Probably because they want girls who cannot bite back, not that my sister ever would.

That would endanger her feeding teeth.

Besides, given her speed and strength, she is more than able to defend herself without ever resorting to fangs.

That is, if it ever came to that, which it likely never will.

Please remember: Julie is by nature, a shy stealthy creature.

Even though she is now an adult, she runs away, rather than fighting or arguing, except of course with me because I am family.

Besides, her nose gives her advanced warning, and being a creature of the night allows her to slip into the darkness and hide with ease, as tourists who come to Hawaii, know for a fact.

Julie meets tour groups that have been screened prior to boarding the bus that takes them to a ranch selected at random by the FBI.

After Julie's short speech and an autograph session, the tourists put on sophisticated night vision glasses and try to keep her in their sights as she heads into the field to feed.

Afterwards, most agree with their tour guide's statement, made before they purchased the tickets, that she is very difficult to see and even harder to track.

Even when the moon is full.

Just as revealing is that the cave she sleeps in, is a completely unlighted twisting maze, deep underground, yet that is where she does her reading assignments before settling down for day sleep.

The end result was and still is, a family life that is indeed different.

I remember during my teenage years, looking up from my homework or returning from a late night date, to find my sister suddenly eyeing at me from some unexpected location, smiling or serious, sometimes with a fang showing, asking: "What is it like to be human?"

I usually responded: "I don't have a clue. Ask mom. She can do the numbers."

Mom is the first to admit that she is just as clueless as dad and I, when it comes to answering that question.

Her advanced degree in Astronomy, supplemented by ample time in Hawaii's observatories, has done little to aid this cause from the astrology standpoint.

As dad notes: "Astronomy and observatory computers are just as clueless when it comes to numerology," so no help there, either.

Still, mom's answer is the best so far.

She states that being human is about being part of a group and an individual, both at the same time.

This, Julie only partly understands.

To her, being part a group is "understandable" in the family sense, but this is something that a solitary hunter cannot relate to.

She sees the world through cat-like one-on-one interactions, versus the pack interactions we humans tend to favor.

This made for a revealing conversation last night.

It began when mom told Julie that the Chinese concept of yin-yang is probably right.

Almost everyone knows the yin-yang symbol of two fishes, one black, one white, nose to tail, endlessly circling, symbolizing constant change, with all possibilities and their concurrent opposites coexisting simultaneously.

Mom used this symbol in an attempt to explain the human need for individuality, noting the individual's insistence upon remaining "the same fish as before," even as they themselves, and the world around them, keeps on spinning and changing.

"Insistence upon this kind of individualism," mom told Julie: "Is why people are so inflexible, yet changeable in their roles and views, and why opposites exist in each person."

The example she used, was: "If a person who is not lazy has a very clean house, their mind might be a mess... or if their mind is organized, then their home might be cluttered."

Julie wondered: "Is that why you feel the need to eat different kinds of foods?"

Dad answered: "Partly, but we also eat a variety of foods because our bodies need the different things that each food type offers."

Mom built on that: "Your need for the same food and our need for a variety of foods is an example of opposites... yin and yang... yet we share the need to eat... and that is what makes people tick. That is... being part of the sameness of a group... while remaining uniquely individual at the same time."

All of us could see that Julie fully understands the words, yet her perception of the world is just differently enough, that the deeper subconscious understanding she wants, eludes her and she has no idea where the gaps are.

Nor do we.

I think this is mostly because she is a vampire.

The only vampire, and she is smart enough to know this, so with a shrug, she noted: "That still does not explain why boys behave the way they do."

I jumped in: "Even I cannot help you, because I have lived around girls all of my life, and I don't fully understand them either..." I smiled: "...or you... but I love Shannon and not having her in my life would be a personal tragedy."

Shannon is my wife, and she often has insights that my sister finds helpful: "Boys are crazy because they have two opposing needs. One is sex. The other is companionship, and each gets in the way of the other, until they finally figure out how to grow up and let pure agape love rule their hearts."

Julie thought about Shannon's words for a while, then spoke the words that her unique need had long ago turned into an everyday idiom: "So where is the cow already?"

This idiom, along with other cow sayings, collectables, and posters, disappoints mom a little, because their popularity long ago eclipsed lighthouses.

Still, mom is a player in this ballpark and she knows her daughter the way only a mother can: "Did you come upon an alluring bull roaming in the pasture?"

After a long moment, my sister confessed: "Two nights ago, I met a guy in the library. When I flashed a fang, he smiled... and his scent is cleaner than any I have ever smelled... and... different?"

Julie seemed to be struggling for words and maybe with her feelings, so Shannon asked: "Nice?"

"Human obviously... but actually... yeah."

Mom had an easy answer: "Get me his full name and birth information, and I will gladly do the charts and numbers."

Printed in the United States
By Bookmasters